The Amazing Story of
Adolphus Tips

Praise for
The Amazing Story of Adolphus Tips

"This is a succinctly engaging tear-jerker, it is also full of happiness and affection and has a joyful ending." *Sunday Times*, Children's Book of the Week

"A heartwarming tale of courage, set during the Second World War, about a cat who survives against the odds." *Independent*

"It's an unshowy yet artfully crafted tale." *Telegraph*

"As always, Morpurgo writes with solid confidence in a voice that's gentle yet spellbinding." *Evening Standard*

"Deceptively simple in tone, Lily's diary reveals the complexities faced by ordinary people caught up in momentous events. This is a story within a story, one that crosses generations to remind us that the events of the past resonate through the years, giving pause for reflection and offering room for hope." *Guardian*, Critic's Choice

"Michael Morpurgo's use of language is impeccable, and the conclusion – both heartbreaking and strange – could not be more satisfying." *Carousel*

michael morpurgo

The Amazing Story of
Adolphus Tips

Illustrated by Michael Foreman

HarperCollins *Children's Books*

Although the evacuation of the South Hams and the practices for D-day actually took place, this novel is a work of fiction. Any reference to real people (living or dead), actual locales and historical events are used solely to lend the fiction an appropriate cultural and historical setting. All other names, characters, places and incidents portrayed in this book are the product of the author's imagination, and any resemblance to actual persons, living or dead, is entirely coincidental.

This edition produced for The Book People Ltd,
Hall Wood Avenue, Haydock, St Helens WA11 9UL

First published in Great Britain by HarperCollins *Children's Books* 2005
HarperCollins *Children's Books* is a division of HarperCollins*Publishers* Ltd
77-85 Fulham Palace Road, Hammersmith, London W6 8JB

The HarperCollins *Children's Books* website address is
www.harpercollinschildrensbooks.co.uk

1

Text copyright © Michael Morpurgo 2005

ISBN 978 0 00 779113 2

The author asserts the moral right to
be identified as the author of the work.

Printed and bound in England by Clays Ltd, St Ives plc

For Ann and Jim Simpson, who brought us to Slapton,
and for their family too, especially Atlanta, Harriet and Effie.

Acknowledgement:
Some of the detail for this story was gleaned from a local history
of Slapton, entitled *The Land Changed its Face* by Grace Bradbeer
(Harbour Books, 1984)

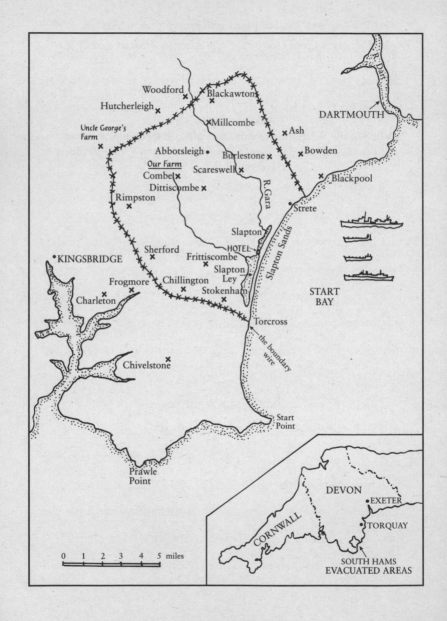

Woodford

Blackawton

Hutcherleigh ×

× Millcombe

DARTMOUTH

Uncle George's
Farm

× Ash

Abbotsleigh •

× Burlestone

Bowden

Our Farm

Scareswell

Combe ×

× Dittiscombe

R. Gara

× Blackpool

Rimpston

Strete •

Slapton

HOTEL

Sherford

KINGSBRIDGE

Frittiscombe

Slapton
Ley

Slapton Sands

Frogmore

Chillington

Stokenham

START
BAY

Charleton

Torcross

the boundary
wire

Chivelstone

Start
Point

Prawle
Point

0 1 2 3 4 5 miles

DEVON

• EXETER

CORNWALL

• TORQUAY

SOUTH HAMS
EVACUATED AREAS

I first read Grandma's letter over ten years ago, when I was twelve. It was the kind of letter you don't forget. I remember I read it over and over again to be sure I'd understood it right. Soon everyone else at home had read it too.

"Well, I'm gobsmacked," my father said.

"She's unbelievable," said my mother.

Grandma rang up later that evening. "Boowie? Is that you, dear? It's Grandma here."

It was Grandma who had first called me Boowie. Apparently Boowie was the first "word" she ever heard me speak. My real name is Michael, but she's never called me that.

"You've read it then?" she went on.

"Yes, Grandma. Is it true – all of it?"

"Of course it is," she said, with a distant echoing chuckle. "Blame it on the cat if you like, Boowie. But remember one thing, dear: only dead fish swim with the flow, and I'm not a dead fish yet, not by a long chalk."

So it was true, all of it. She'd really gone and done it. I

felt like whooping and cheering, like jumping up and down for joy. But everyone else still looked as if they were in a state of shock. All day, aunties and uncles and cousins had been turning up and there'd been lots of tutting and shaking of heads and mutterings.

"What does she think she's doing?"

"And at her age!"

"Grandpa's only been dead a few months."

"Barely cold in his grave."

And, to be fair, Grandpa *had* only been dead a few months: five months and two weeks to be precise.

It had rained cats and dogs all through the funeral service, so loud you could hardly hear the organ sometimes. I remember some baby began crying and had to be taken out. I sat next to Grandma in the front pew, right beside the coffin. Grandma's hand was trembling, and when I looked up at her she smiled and squeezed my arm to tell me she was all right. But I knew she wasn't, so I held her hand. Afterwards we walked down the aisle together behind the coffin, holding on tightly to one another.

Then we were standing under her umbrella by the

graveside and watching them lower the coffin, the vicar's words whipped away by the wind before they could ever be heard. I remember I tried hard to feel sad, but I couldn't, and not because I didn't love Grandpa. I did. But he had been ill with multiple sclerosis for ten years or more, and that was most of my life. So I'd never felt I'd known him that well. When I was little he'd sit by my bed and read stories to me. Later I did the same for him. Sometimes it was all he could do to smile. In the end, when he was really bad, Grandma had to do almost everything for him. She even had to interpret what he was trying to say to me because I couldn't understand any more. In the last few holidays I spent down at Slapton I could see the suffering in his eyes. He hated being the way he was, and he hated me seeing the way he was too. So when I heard he'd died I was sad for Grandma, of course – they'd been married for over forty years. But in a way I was glad it was finished, for her and for him.

After the burial was over we walked back together along the lane to the pub for the wake, Grandma still clutching my hand. I didn't feel I should say anything to her in case I disturbed her thoughts. So I left her alone.

We were walking under the bridge, the pub already in sight, when she spoke at last. "He's out of it now, Boowie," she said, "and out of that wheelchair too. God, how he hated that wheelchair. He'll be happy again now. You should've seen him before, Boowie. You should have known him like I knew him. Strapping great fellow he was, and gentle too, always kind. He tried to stay kind, right to the end. We used to laugh in the early days – how we used to laugh. That was the worst of it in a way; he just stopped laughing a long time ago, when he first got ill. That's why I always loved having you to stay, Boowie. You reminded me of how he had been when he was young. You were always laughing, just like he used to in the old days, and that made me feel good. It made Grandpa feel good too. I know it did."

This wasn't like Grandma at all. Normally with Grandma I was the one who did the talking. She never said much, she just listened. I'd confided in her all my life. I don't know why, but I found I could always talk to her easily, much more easily than with anyone at home. Back home, people were always busy. Whenever I talked to them I'd feel I was interrupting something. With Grandma

I knew I had her total attention. She made me feel I was the only person in the world who mattered to her.

Ever since I could remember I'd been coming down to Slapton for my holidays, mostly on my own. Grandma's bungalow was more of a home to me than anywhere, because we'd moved house often – too often for my liking. I'd just get used to things, settle down, make a new set of friends and then we'd be off, on the move again. Slapton summers with Grandma were regular and reliable and I loved the sameness of them, and Harley in particular.

Grandma used to take me out in secret on Grandpa's beloved motorbike, his pride and joy, an old Harley-Davidson. We called it Harley. Before Grandpa became ill they would go out on Harley whenever they could, which wasn't often. She told me once those were the happiest times they'd had together. Now that he was too ill to take her out on Harley, she'd take me instead. We'd tell Grandpa all about it, of course, and he liked to hear exactly where we'd been, what field we'd stopped in for our picnic and how fast we'd gone. I'd relive it for him and he loved that. But we never told my family. It was to be our secret, Grandma said, because if anyone back home ever got to know she took me out on Harley they'd never let me come to stay again. She was right too. I had the impression that neither my father (her own son) nor my mother really saw eye to eye with Grandma. They always thought she was a bit stubborn, eccentric, irresponsible even. They'd be sure to think that my going out on Harley with her was far too dangerous. But it wasn't. I never felt unsafe on Harley, no matter how fast we went. The faster the better. When we got back, breathless with excitement, our faces numb from the wind, she'd always say the same thing: "Supreme, Boowie! Wasn't that just supreme?"

When we weren't out on Harley, we'd go on long walks down to the beach and fly kites, and on the way back we'd watch the moorhens and coots and herons on Slapton Ley. We saw a bittern once. "Isn't that supreme?" Grandma whispered in my ear. Supreme was always her favourite word for anything she loved: for motorbikes or birds or lavender. The house always smelt of lavender. Grandma adored the smell of it, the colour of it. Her soap was always lavender, and there was a sachet in every wardrobe and chest of drawers – to keep moths away, she said.

Best of all, even better than clinging on to Grandma as

we whizzed down the deep lanes on Harley, were the wild and windy days when the two of us would stomp noisily along the pebble beach of Slapton Sands, clutching on to one another so we didn't get blown away. We could never be gone for long though, because of Grandpa. He was happy enough to be left on his own for a while, but only if there was sport on the television. So we would generally go off for our ride on Harley or on one of our walks when there was a cricket match on, or rugby. He liked rugby best. He had been good at it himself when he was younger, very good, Grandma said proudly. He'd even played for Devon from time to time – whenever he could get away from the farm, that is.

Grandma had told me a little about the busy life they'd had before I was born, up on the farm – she'd taken me up there to show me. So I knew how they'd milked a herd of sixty South Devon cows and that Grandpa had gone on working as long as he could. In the end, as his illness took hold and he couldn't go up and down stairs any more, they'd had to sell up the farm and the animals and move into the bungalow down in Slapton village. Mostly, though, she'd want to talk about me, ask about me, and she really wanted to know, too. Maybe it was because I was her only grandson. She never seemed to judge me either. So there was nothing I didn't tell her about my life at home or my friends or my worries. She never gave advice, she just listened.

Once, I remember, she told me that whenever I came to stay it made her feel younger. "The older I get," she said, "the more I want to be young. That's why I love going out on Harley. And I'm going to go on being young till I drop, no matter what."

I understood well enough what she meant by "no matter what". Each time I'd gone down in the last couple of years before Grandpa died she had looked more grey and weary. I would often hear my father pleading with her to have Grandpa put into a nursing home, that she couldn't go on looking after him on her own any longer. Sometimes the pleading sounded more like bullying to me, and I wished he'd stop. Anyway, Grandma wouldn't hear of it. She did have a nurse who came in to bath Grandpa each day now, but Grandma had to do the rest all by herself, and she was becoming exhausted. More and more of my walks along the beach were alone nowadays. We couldn't go out on Harley at all. She couldn't leave Grandpa even for ten minutes without him fretting, without her worrying about him. But after Grandpa was in bed we would either play Scrabble, which she would let me win sometimes, or we'd talk on late into the night – or rather I would talk and she would listen. Over the years I reckon I must have given Grandma a running commentary on just about my entire life, from the first moment I could speak, all the way through my childhood.

But now, after Grandpa's funeral, as we walked

together down the road to the pub with everyone following behind us, it was her turn to do the talking, and she was talking about herself, talking nineteen to the dozen, as she'd never talked before. Suddenly I was the listener.

The wake in the pub was crowded, and of course everyone wanted to speak to Grandma, so we didn't get a chance to talk again that day, not alone. I was playing waiter with the tea and coffee, and plates of quiches and cakes. When we left for home that evening Grandma hugged me especially tight, and afterwards she touched my cheek as she'd always done when she was saying good night to me before she switched off the light. She wasn't crying, not quite. She whispered to me as she held me. "Don't you worry about me, Boowie dear," she said. "There's times it's good to be on your own. I'll go for rides on Harley – Harley will help me feel better. I'll be fine." So we drove away and left her with the silence of her empty house all around her.

A few weeks later she came to us for Christmas, but she seemed very distant, almost as if she were lost inside herself: there, but not there somehow. I thought she must still be grieving and I knew that was private, so I left her alone and we didn't talk much. Yet, strangely, she didn't seem too sad. In fact she looked serene, very calm and still, a dreamy smile on her face, as if she was happy enough to be there, just so long as she didn't have to join in too much. I'd often find her sitting and gazing into space, remembering a Christmas with Grandpa perhaps, I thought, or maybe a Christmas down on the farm when she was growing up.

On Christmas Day itself, after lunch, she said she wanted to go for a walk. So we went off to the park, just the two of us. We were sitting watching the ducks on the pond when she told me. "I'm going away, Boowie," she said. "It'll be in the New Year, just for a while."

"Where to?" I asked her.

"I'll tell you when I get there," she replied. "Promise. I'll send you a letter."

She wouldn't tell me any more no matter how much I badgered her. We took her to the station a couple of days later and waved her off. Then there was silence. No letter, no postcard, no phone call. A week went by. A fortnight. No one else seemed to be that concerned about her, but I was. We all knew she'd gone travelling, she'd made no secret of it, although she'd told no one where she was going. But she had promised to write to me and nothing had come. Grandma never broke her promises. Never. Something had gone wrong, I was sure of it.

Then one Saturday morning I picked up the post from the front door mat. There was one for me. I recognised her handwriting at once. The envelope was quite heavy too. Everyone else was soon busy reading their own post, but I wanted to open Grandma's envelope in private. So I ran upstairs to my room, sat on the bed and opened it. I pulled out what looked more like a manuscript than a letter, about thirty or forty pages long at least, closely typed. On the cover page she had sellotaped a black and white photograph (more brown and white really) of a small girl who looked a lot like me, smiling toothily into the camera and cradling a large black and white cat in her arms. There was a title: *The Amazing Story of Adolphus Tips*, with her name underneath, Lily Tregenza. Attached to the manuscript by a large multicoloured paperclip was this letter.

Dearest Boowie,

This is the only way I could think of to explain to you properly why I've done what I've done. I'll have told you some of this already over the years, but now I want you to know the whole story. Some people will think I'm mad, perhaps most people — I don't mind that. But you won't think I'm mad, not when you've read this. You'll understand, I know you will. That's why I particularly wanted you to read it first. You can show it to everyone else afterwards. I'll phone soon... when you're over the surprise.

When I was about your age — and by the way that's me on the front cover with Tips — I used to keep a diary. I was an only child, so I'd talk to myself in my diary. It was company for me, almost like a friend. So what you'll be reading is the story of my life as it happened, beginning in the autumn of 1943, during the Second World War, when I was growing up on the family farm. I'll be honest with you, I've done quite a lot of editing. I've left bits out here and there because some of it was too private or too boring or too long. I used to write pages and pages sometimes, just talking to myself, rambling on.

The surprise comes right at the very end. So don't cheat, Boowie. Don't look at the end. Let it be a surprise for you — as it still is for me.

Lots of love,

Grandma

PS Harley must be feeling very lonely all on his own in the garage. We'll go for a ride as soon as I get back; as soon as you come to visit. Promise.

THE AMAZING STORY OF ADOLPHUS TIPS

Lily Tregenza

Friday, September 10th 1943

I've been back at school a whole week now. When Miss McAllister left at the end of last term I was cock-a-hoop (I like that word), we all were. She was a witch, I'm sure she was. I thought everything would be tickety-boo (I like that word too) just perfect, and I was so much looking forward to school without her. And who do we get as a head teacher instead? Mrs "Bloomers" Blumfeld. She's all smiles on the outside, but underneath she's an even worser witch than Miss McAllister. I know I'm not supposed to say worser but it sounds worser than worse, so I'm using it. So there. We call her Bloomers because of her name of course, and also because she came into class once with her skirt hitched up by mistake in her navy-blue bloomers.

Today Bloomers gave me a detention just because my hands were dirty again. "Lily Tregenza, I think you are one of the most untidiest girls I have ever known." She can't even say her words properly. She says zink instead of think and de instead of the. She can't even speak English properly and she's supposed to be our teacher. So I said it wasn't fair, and she gave me another detention. I hate her accent; she could be German. Maybe she's a spy! She looks like a spy. I hate her, I really do. And what's more, she favours the townies, the evacuees. That's because she's come down from London like they have. She told us so.

We've got three more townies in my class this term, all from London like the others. There's so many of them now there's hardly enough room to play in the playground. There's almost as many of them as there are of us. They're always fighting too. Most of them are all right, I suppose, except that they talk funny. I can't understand half of what they say. And they stick together too much. They look at us sometimes like we've got measles or mumps or something, like they think we're all stupid country bumpkins, which we're not.

One of the new ones – Barry Turner he's called – is living in Mrs Morwhenna's house, next to the shop. He's got red hair everywhere, even red eyebrows. And he picks his nose which is disgusting. He gets lots more spellings wrong than me, but Bloomers never gives *him* a detention. I know why too. It's because Barry's dad was killed in the airforce at Dunkirk. My dad's away in the army, and he's alive. So just because he's not dead, I get a detention. Is that fair? Barry told Maisie, who sits next to me in class now and who's my best friend sometimes, that she could kiss him if she wanted to. He's only been at our school a week. Cheeky monkey. Maisie said she let him because he's young – he's only ten – and because she was sorry for him, on account of his dad, and also because she wanted to find out if townies were any good at it. She said it was a bit sticky but all right. I don't do kissing. I don't see the point of it, not if it's sticky.

Tips is going to have her kittens any day now. She's all saggy baggy underneath. Last time she had them on my bed. She's the best cat (and the biggest) in the whole wide world and I love her more than anyone or anything. But she keeps having kittens, and I wish she wouldn't because we can't ever keep them. No one wants them because everyone's got cats of their own already, and they all have kittens too.

It was all because of Tips and her kittens that I had my row with Dad, the biggest row of my life, when he was last home on leave from the army. He did it when I was at school, without even telling me. As soon as they were born he took all her kittens out and drowned them just like that. When I found out I said terrible things to him, like I would never ever speak to him again and how I hoped the Germans would kill him. I was horrible to him. I never made it up with him either. I wrote him a letter saying I was sorry, but he hasn't replied and I wish he would. He probably hates me now, and I wouldn't blame him. If anything happened to him I couldn't bear it, not after what I said.

Mum keeps telling me I shouldn't let my tongue do my thinking for me, and I'm not quite sure what that means. She's just come in to say good night and blow out my lamp. She says I spend too much time writing my diary. She thinks I can't write in the dark, but I can. My writing may look a bit wonky in the morning, but I don't care.

Sunday, September 12th 1943

We saw some American soldiers in Slapton today; it's the first time I've ever seen them. Everyone calls them Yanks, I don't know why. Grandfather doesn't like them, but I do. I think they've got smarter uniforms than ours and they look bigger somehow. They smiled a lot and waved – particularly at Mum, but that was just because she's pretty, I could tell. When they whistled she went very red, but she liked it. They don't say "hello", they say "hi" instead, and one of them said "howdy". He was the one who gave me a sweet, only he called it "candy". I'm sucking it now as I'm writing. It's nice, but not as nice as lemon sherberts or peppermint humbugs with the stripes and chewy centres. Humbugs are my best favourites, but I'm only allowed two a week now because of rationing. Mum says we're really lucky living on the farm because we can grow our own vegetables, make our own milk and butter and cream and eat our own chickens. So when I complain about sweet rationing, which I do, she always gives me a little lecture on how lucky we are. Barry says they've got rationing for everything in London, so maybe Mum is right. Maybe we are lucky. But I still don't see how me having less peppermint humbugs is going to help us win the war.

Thursday, September 16th 1943

Mum got a letter from Dad today. Whenever she gets a letter she's very happy and sad at the same time. She says he's out in the desert in Africa with the Eighth Army and he's making sure the lorries and the tanks work – he's very good at engines, my dad. It's very hot in the daytime, he says, but at night it's cold enough to freeze your toes off. Mum let me read the letter after she had. He didn't say anything about Tips and the kittens or the row we had. Maybe he's forgotten all about it. I hope so.

I feel bad about writing this, but I must write what I really feel. What's the point in writing at all otherwise? The truth is, I don't really miss Dad like I know I should, like I know Mum does. When I'm actually reading his letters I miss him lots, but then later on I forget all about him unless someone talks about him, unless I see his photo maybe. Perhaps it's because I'm still cross with him about the kittens. But it's not just because of the kittens that I'm cross with him. The thing is, he didn't need to go to fight in the war; he could have stayed with us and helped Grandfather and Mum on the farm. Other farmers were allowed to stay. *He* could have. But he didn't. He tried to explain it to me before he joined up. He said he wouldn't feel right about staying home when there were so many men going off to the war, men the same age as he was. I told him he should think of Grandfather and Mum and me, but he wouldn't listen. They've got to do all the work on their own now, all the milking and the muck spreading, all the haymaking and the lambing. Dad was the only one who could fix his Fordson tractor and the thresher, and now he's not here to do it. I help out a bit, but I'm not much use. I'm only twelve (almost anyway) and I'm off to school most days. He should be here with us, that's what I think. I'm fed up with him being away. I'm fed up with this war. We're not allowed down on the beach any more to fly our kites. There's barbed wire all around it to keep us off, and there's mines buried all over it. They've put horrible signs up everywhere warning us off. That wasn't much use to Farmer Jeffrey's smelly old one-eyed sheepdog that lifted his leg on everything he passed (including my leg once). He wandered on to the beach under the wire yesterday and blew himself up. Poor old thing.

I had this idea at school (probably because Bloomers was reading us the King Arthur stories). I think we should dress Churchill and Hitler up in armour like King Arthur's knights, stick them on horses, give them a lance each and let them sort it out between them. Whoever is knocked off loses, and the war would be over and we could all go back to being normal again. Churchill would win of course, because Hitler looks too weak and feeble even to sit on a horse, let alone hold a lance. So we would win. No more rationing. All the humbugs I want. Dad could come home and everything would be like it was before. Everything would be tickety-boo.

Friday, September 17th 1943

I saw a fox this morning running across south field with a hen in his mouth. When I shouted at him, he stopped and looked at me for a moment as if he was telling me to mind my own business. Then he just trotted off, cool as you like, without a care in the world. Mum says it wasn't one of her hens, but she was someone's hen, wasn't she? Someone should tell that fox about rationing. That's what I think.

There's lots of daddy-longlegs crawling up my window, and a butterfly. I'll just let them out...

It's still light outside. I love light evenings. It was a red admiral butterfly. Beautiful. Supreme.

Mum and Grandfather are having an argument downstairs, I can hear them. Grandfather is going on about the American soldiers again, "ruddy Yanks" he calls them. He says they're all over the place, hundreds of them, and walking about as if they own the place, smoking cigars, chewing gum. Like an invasion, he says. Mum speaks more quietly than Grandfather, so it's difficult to hear what she's saying.

They've stopped arguing now. They've got the radio on instead. I don't know why they bother. The news of the war is always bad, and it only makes them feel miserable. It's hardly ever off, that radio.

Monday, September 20th 1943

Two big surprises. One good, one bad. We were all sent home from school today. That was the good one. It was all because of Mr Adolf Ruddy Hitler, as Grandfather calls him. So thanks for the holiday, Mr Adolf Ruddy Hitler. We were sitting doing arithmetic with Bloomers – long division which I can't understand no matter how hard I try – when we heard the roaring and rumbling of an aeroplane overhead, getting louder and louder, and the classroom windows started to rattle. Then there was this huge explosion and the whole school shook. We all got down on the floor and crawled under the desks like we have to do in air-raid practice, except this was very much more exciting because it was real. By the time Bloomers had got us out into the playground the German bomber was already far out over the sea. We could see the black crosses on its wings. Barry pretended he was firing an ack-ack gun and tried to shoot it

down. Most of the boys joined in, making their silly machine-gun noises – dadadadadada.

Bloomers sent us home just in case there were more bombers on the way. But we didn't go home. Instead we all went off to see if we could find where the bomb had landed. We found it too. There was a massive hole in Mr Berry's cornfield just outside the village. The Home Guard was there already, Uncle George in his uniform telling them all what to do. They were making sure no one fell in, I suppose. No one had been hurt, except a poor old pigeon who was probably having a good feed of corn when the bomb fell. His feathers were everywhere. Then one of the townies got all hoity-toity about it and said he'd seen much bigger holes than this one back home, in London. Big Ned Simmons told him just where he could go and just what he thought of him and all the snotty-nosed townies, and it all got a bit nasty after that, us against them. So I walked away.

I was on my way home afterwards when I saw this jeep coming down the lane towards me. There was one soldier in it. He had an American helmet on. He screeched to a stop and said, "Hi there!" He was a black man. I've never in my life seen a black person before, only in pictures in books, so I didn't quite know what to say. I kept trying not to stare, but I couldn't help myself. He had to ask me twice if he was on the right road to Torpoint before I even managed a nod. "You know something? You got pigtails just like my littlest sister." Then he said, "See ya!" and off he went, splashing through the puddles. I was a bit disappointed not to get any candy.

When I got home I had my other surprise, my bad one. I told them about the bomb and about Uncle George and the Home Guard being there, and I told them about the black soldier I'd met in the lane. They didn't seem very interested in any of it. I thought that was strange. And it was strange too that neither of them seemed to want to talk to me much or even to look at me. We were all having tea in the kitchen when Tips came in. She rubbed herself against my leg and then went off mewing under the table, under the dresser, into the pantry. But she wasn't mewing like she does when she's after food or love, or when she brings in a mouse. She was calling, and when I picked her up she felt different. Still saggy baggy underneath, but definitely different. She wasn't full and fat any more. I knew what they'd done at once.

"We had to do it, Lily," Mum said. "It's better straight away, before she gets too fond of them. Sometimes you have to be cruel to be kind."

I screamed at them: "Murderers! Murderers!" Then I brought Tips up to my room. I'm still up here with her now. I've been crying ever since, and really loudly too so they can hear me, so they'll feel really bad, as bad as I do.

Tips is lying in my lap and washing herself just like nothing's happened. She's even purring. Maybe she doesn't know yet. Or maybe she does and she's forgiven us already. Now she's stopped licking herself. She's looking at me as if she knows. I don't think she has forgiven us. I don't think she'll ever forgive us. Why should she?

Tuesday, October 5th 1943

My birthday. I was born twelve years ago today at ten o'clock in the morning. I've been calling myself twelve for a long time, and now I really am. All I want to be now is thirteen. And even thirteen isn't old enough. I so much want to be much older than I am, but not old like Grandfather so that I walk bent and my hands are all hard and wrinkly and veiny. I don't want a drippy nose and hairs growing out of my ears. But I do want the years to hurry on by until I'm about seventeen, so school and Bloomers and long division are over and done with, so that no one can take my kittens away and drown them. It'll be so good when I'm seventeen, because the war will be over by then, that's for sure. Grandfather says that we're already winning and so it can't be long till it's finished. Then I can go up to London on the train – I've never been on a train – and I can see the shops and ride on those big red buses and go on the underground. Barry

Turner's told me all about it. He says there's lights in the streets, millions of people everywhere, and cinemas and dance halls. His dad used to work in a cinema before the war, before he was killed. He told me that one day. That was the first thing he's ever told me about his dad.

Which reminds me: I still haven't had a letter from *my* dad. I think he's still cross with me after what I said. I wish, I wish I hadn't said it. I had a dream about him the other night. I don't usually remember my dreams at all, but I remember this one, some of it anyway. He was back at home milking cows again, but he was in uniform with his tin helmet on. It was scary because, when I came into the milking parlour, I spoke to him and he never looked up. I shouted but he still never looked at me. It was like one of us wasn't there, but we were. We both were.

Monday, November 1st 1943

"Pinch, punch, first day of the month. Slap and a kick for being so quick. Punch in the eye for being so sly." Barry kept saying it to me every time he saw me. It was really annoying. In the end I shouted at him and hurt his feelings. I know I shouldn't have, he was only trying to be friendly. He didn't cry but he nearly did.

But tonight I feel worse about something else, something much worse. Ever since Bloomers came I've been giving her a hard time, we all have, but me most of all. I'm really good at giving people a hard time when I want to. I cheeked her when she first came because I didn't like her and she got ratty and punished me. So I cheeked her again and she punished me again and on it went, and after that I could never get on with her at all. I've been mean to her ever since I've known her, and now this has happened.

The vicar came into school today and told us

he'd be teaching us for the morning because Mrs Blumfeld wasn't feeling very well. She wasn't ill so much as sad, he said, sad because she had just heard the news that her husband, who is in the merchant navy, had been lost at sea in the Atlantic. His ship had been torpedoed. They'd picked up a few survivors, but Mrs Blumfeld's husband wasn't one of them. The vicar told us that when she came back into school we had to be very good and kind, so as not to upset her. Then he said we should close our eyes and hold our hands together and pray for her. I did pray for her too, but I also prayed for myself, because I don't want God to have his own back on me for all the horrible things I've said and thought about her. I prayed for my dad too, that God wouldn't make him die in the desert just because I'd been mean to Mrs Blumfeld, that I hadn't meant it when I'd said I wanted him to die because he drowned the kittens. I've never prayed so hard in my life. Usually my mind wanders when I'm supposed to be praying, but it didn't today.

After lunch Mrs Blumfeld came into school. She had no lipstick on. She looked so pale and cold. She was trembling a little too. We left a letter for her on her desk which we had all signed, to say how sorry we all were about her husband. She looked very calm, as if she was in a daze. She wasn't crying or anything, not until she read our letter. Then she tried to smile at us through her tears and said it was very thoughtful of us, which it wasn't because it was the vicar's idea, but we didn't tell her that. We all went around whispering and being extra good and quiet all day. I feel so bad for her now because she's all alone. I won't call her Bloomers ever again. I don't think anyone will.

Monday, November 8th 1943

Ever since Mrs Blumfeld's husband was killed, I've been worrying a lot about Dad. I didn't before, but I am now, all the time. I keep thinking of him lying dead in the sand of Africa. I try not to, but the picture of him lying there keeps coming into my head. And it's silly, I know it is, because I got a letter from him only yesterday, at last, and he's fine. (His letters take for ever to come. This one was dated two months ago.) He never said anything about me being cross. In fact he sent his love to Tips. Dad says it's so hot out in the desert he could almost fry an egg on the bonnet of his jeep. He says he longs for a few days of good old Devon drizzle, and mud. He really misses mud. How can you miss mud? We're all sick of mud. It's been raining here for days now: mizzly, drizzly, horrible rain. Today it was blowing in from the sea, so I was wet through by the time I got home from school.

Grandfather came in later. He'd been drinking a

bit, but then he always drinks a bit when he goes to market, just to keep the cold out, he says. He sat down in front of the stove and put his feet in the bottom oven to warm up. Mum hates him doing it but he does it all the same. He's got holes in his socks too. He always has.

"There's hundreds of gum-chewing Yanks everywhere in town," he said. "Like flies on a ruddy cow clap." I like it when Grandfather talks like that. He got a dirty look from Mum, but he didn't mind. He just gave me a big wink and a wicked grin and went on talking. He said he was sure something's going on: there are fuel dumps everywhere you look, tents going up all over the place, tanks and lorries parked everywhere. "It's something big," he said. "I'm telling you."

Still raining out there. It's lashing the windowpanes as I'm writing, and the whole house is creaking and shaking, almost as if it's getting ready to take off and fly out over the sea. I can hear the cows lowing in the barn. They're scared. Tips is frightened silly too. She wants to hide. She keeps jogging my writing. She's trying to push her head deeper and deeper into my armpit. *I'm* not frightened, I like storms. I like it when the sea comes thundering in and the wind blows so hard that it takes your breath away.

Mrs Blumfeld said something this morning that took my breath away too. That Daisy Simmons, Ned's little sister, is always asking questions when she shouldn't and today she put her hand up and asked Mrs Blumfeld if she was a mummy, just like that! Mrs Blumfeld didn't seem to mind at all. She thought for a bit, then she said that she would never have any children of her own because she didn't need them; she had all of us instead. We were her family now. And she had her cats, which she loved. I didn't know she had cats. I was watching her when she said it and you could see she really did love them. I was so wrong about her. She likes cats so she must be nice. I'm going to sleep now and I'm not going to think of Dad lying out in the desert. I'm going to think of Mrs Blumfeld at home with her cats instead.

I just went to shut the window, and I saw a barn owl flying across the farmyard, white and silent in the darkness. There one moment, gone the next. A ghost owl. He's screeching now. They screech, they don't toowit-toowoo. That word looks really funny when you write it down, but owls don't have to write it down, do they? They just have to hoot it, or toowit-toowoo it.

Saturday, November 13th 1943

Today was a day that will change my life for ever.

Grandfather was right when he said something was up. And it is something big too, something very big – I have to keep pinching myself to believe it's true, that it's really going to happen. Yesterday was just like any other day. Rain. School. Long division. Spelling test. Barry picking his nose. Barry smiling at me from across the classroom with his big round eyes. I just wish he wouldn't smile at me so. He's always so smiley.

Then today it happened. I knew all day there was going to be some kind of meeting in the church in the evening, that someone from every house had to go and it was important. I knew that, because Mum and Grandfather were arguing about it over breakfast before I went off to school. Grandfather was being a grumpy old goat. He's been getting crotchety a lot just lately. (Mum says it's because of his rheumatism – it gets worse in damp weather.) He kept saying he had too much to do on the farm to be bothered with meetings and such. And besides, he said, women were better at talking because they did more of it. Of course that made Mum really mad, so they had a fair old ding-dong about it. Anyway in the end Mum gave in and said she'd go, and she asked me to go along with her for company. I didn't want to go but now I'm glad I did, really glad.

The place was packed out. There was standing room only by the time we got there. Then this bigwig, Lord Somethingorother, got up and started talking. I didn't pay much attention at first because he had this droning-on hoity-toity (I like that word) sort of voice that almost put me to sleep. But suddenly I felt a strange stillness and silence all around me. It was almost as if everyone had stopped breathing. Everyone was listening, so I listened too. I can't remember his exact words, but I think it went something like this.

"I know it's asking a lot of you," the bigwig was saying, "but I promise we wouldn't be asking you if we didn't have to, if it wasn't absolutely necessary. They'll be needing the beach at Slapton Sands and the whole area behind it, including this village. They need it because they have to practise landings from the sea for the invasion of France when it comes. That's all I can tell you. Everything else is top secret. No point in asking me anything about it, because I don't know any more than you do. What I do know is that you have seven weeks from today to move out, lock, stock and barrel – and I mean that. You have to take everything with you: furniture, food, coal, all your animals, farm machinery, fuel, and all fodder and crops that can

be carried. Nothing you value must be left behind. After the seven weeks is up, no one will be allowed back – and I mean no one. There'll be a barbed-wire perimeter fence and guards everywhere to keep you out. Besides which, it will be dangerous. There'll be live firing going on: real shells, real bullets. I know it's hard, but don't imagine it's just Slapton, that you're the only ones. Torcross, East Allington, Stokenham, Sherford, Chillington, Strete, Blackawton: 3000 people have got to move out; 750 families, 30,000 acres of land have got to be cleared in seven weeks."

Some people tried to stand up and ask questions, but it was no use. He just waved them down.

"I've told you. It's no good asking me the whys and wherefores. All I know is what I've told you. They need it for the war effort, for training purposes. That's all you need to know."

"Yes, but for how long?" asked the vicar from the back of the hall.

"About six months, nine months, maybe longer.

We can't be sure. And don't worry. We'll make sure everyone has a place to live, and of course there'll be proper compensation paid to everyone, to all the farms and businesses for any loss or damage. And I have to be honest with you here, I have to warn you that there will be damage, lots of it."

You could have heard a pin drop. I was expecting lots of protests and questions, but everyone seemed to be struck dumb. I looked up at Mum. She was staring ahead of her, her mouth half open, her face pale. All the way home in the dark, I kept asking her questions, but she never said a word till we reached the farmyard.

"It'll kill him," she whispered. "Your grandfather. It'll kill him."

Once back home she came straight out with it. Grandfather was in his chair warming his toes in the oven as usual. "We've got to clear out," she said, and she told him the whole thing. Grandfather was silent for a moment or two. Then he just said, "They'll have to carry me out first. I was born here and I'll die here. I'm not moving, not for they ruddy Yanks, not for no one." Mum's still downstairs with him, trying to persuade him. But he won't listen. I know he won't. Grandfather doesn't say all that much, but what he says he means. What he says, he sticks to. Tips has jumped up on my bed and walked all over my diary with her muddy paws! She's lucky I love her as much as I do.

Tuesday, November 16th 1943

At school, in the village, no matter where you go or whoever you meet, it's all anyone talks about: the evacuation. It's like a sudden curse has come down on us all. No one smiles. No one's the same. There's been a thick fog ever since we were told. It hangs all around us, tries to come in at the windows. It makes me wonder if it'll ever go away, if we'll ever see the sun again.

I've changed my mind completely about Barry. That skunkhead Bob Bolan came up to me at playtime and started on about Grandfather, just because he's the only one in the village refusing to go. He said he was a stupid old duffer. He said he should be sent away to a lunatic asylum and locked up. Maisie was there with me and *she* never stood up for me, and I thought she was supposed to be my best friend. Well she's not, not any more. No one stood up for me, so I had to stand up for myself. I pushed Skunkhead (I won't call him Bob any more because Skunkhead suits him better) and Skunkhead pushed me, and I fell over and grazed my elbow. I was sitting there, picking the grit out of my skin and trying not to let them see I was crying, when Barry came up. The next thing I know he's got Skunkhead on the ground and he's punching him. Mrs Blumfeld had to pull him off, but not before Skunkhead got a bleeding nose, which served him right. As she took them both back into school Barry looked over his shoulder and smiled. I never got a chance to say thank you, but I will. If only he'd stop picking his nose and smiling at me I think I could really like him a lot. But I'm not doing kissing with him.

Tuesday, November 30th 1943

Some people have started moving their things out already. This morning I saw Maisie's dad going up the road with a cartload of beds and chairs, cupboards, tea chests and all sorts. Maisie was sitting on the top and waving at me. She's my friend again, but not my best friend. I think Barry's my best friend now because I know I can really trust him. Then I saw Miss Langley driving off in a car with lots of cases and trunks strapped on top. She had Jimbo on her lap, her horrible Jack Russell dog who chases Tips up trees whenever he sees her. Mum told me that Miss Langley is off to stay with a cousin up in Scotland, hundreds of miles away. I've just told Tips and suddenly she's purring very happily. It's a "good riddance" purr, I think.

A lot of people are going to stay with relatives, and we could too except that Grandfather won't hear of it. Uncle George farms only a couple of miles away, just beyond where the wire fence will be. They're beginning to put it up already. He said that family's family, and he'd be only too happy to help us out. I heard him telling Grandfather. We could take our milking cows up to his place, all our sheep, all the farm machinery, Dad's Fordson tractor, everything. It'll be a tight squeeze, Uncle George said, but we could manage. Grandfather won't listen. He won't leave, and that's that.

Wednesday, December 1st 1943

At playtime I found Barry sitting on his own on the dustbins behind the bike shed. He was all red around the eyes. He'd been crying, but he was trying not to show it. He wouldn't tell me why at first, but after a while I got it out of him. It's because there won't be room for him any more with Mrs Morwhenna when she moves into Kingsbridge next week. He likes her a lot and now he has nowhere to go. So, to make him feel better, and because of what he had done for me the other day with Skunkhead, I said he could come home with me and play after school, so long as he didn't pick his nose. He perked up after that, and he was even chirpier when he saw the cows and the sheep. And when he saw Dad's Fordson tractor he went loopy. It was like he'd been given a new toy of his own to play with. I couldn't get him off it. Grandfather took him off around the farm, letting him steer the tractor – which wasn't fair because he's never let me do that. By the time they came back they were both of them as happy as larks. I haven't heard Grandfather laugh so much in ages.

Barry tucked into Mum's cream sponge cake, slice after slice of it, and all the time he never stopped talking about the tractor and the farm (and no one told him not to talk with his mouth full, which wasn't fair either because Mum's always ticking me off for that). He'd have scoffed the lot if Mum hadn't taken it away. He still smiles at me, but I don't mind so much now. In fact I quite like it really.

Afterwards, when we were walking together down the lane to the farm gate, he seemed suddenly down in the dumps. He hardly said a word all the way. Then suddenly he just blurted it out. "I could come and stay," he said. "I wouldn't be a nuisance, honest. I wouldn't pick my nose, honest." I couldn't say no, but I didn't want to say yes, not exactly. I mean, it would be like having a brother in the house. I'd never had a brother and I wasn't sure I wanted one, even if Barry was my best friend now, sort of. So I said maybe. I said I'd ask. And I did, at supper time. Grandfather didn't even have to think about it. "The lad needs a home, doesn't he?" he said. "We've got a home. He needs feeding. We've got food. We should have had one of those evacuee children before, but I never liked townies much till now. This one's all right though. He's a good lad. Besides, it'll be good to have a boy about the place. Be like the old days, when your father was a boy. You tell him he can come."

He never asked me what I thought, never asked Mum. He just said yes. It took me so much by surprise that I wasn't ready for it, and neither was Mum. So it looks as if I'm going to have a sort of brother living with us, whether I like it or not. Mum came in a minute ago and sat on my bed. "Do you mind about Barry?" she asked me.

"He's all right, I suppose," I told her. And he is too, except when he's picking his nose of course.

"One thing's for sure, it'll make Grandfather happier," Mum said. "And if he's happier, then maybe it'll be easier to talk him into leaving, into moving to Uncle George's place. They're going to move us out, you know, Lily. One way or another, they're going to do it." She gave me a good long cuddle tonight. She hasn't done that for ages. I think she thinks I'm too old for it or something, but I'm not.

I haven't had my nightmare about Dad for a long time now, which is good. But I haven't thought much about him either, which is not so good.

Wednesday, December 15th 1943

Barry moved in this afternoon. He walked home with me from school carrying his suitcase. He skipped most of the way. He's sleeping in the room at the end of the passage. Grandfather says that's where Dad always used to sleep when he was a boy. Straight after tea Grandfather took him out to feed the cows. From the look on Barry's face when he came back I'm sure he thinks he's in heaven. Like he says, there's no tractors in London, no cows, no sheep, no pigs. He's already decided he likes the sheep best. And he likes mud too, and he likes rolling down hills and getting his coat covered in sheep poo. He told Mum that brown's his favourite colour because he likes mud, and sausages. I learnt a little bit more about him today – he tells Mum more than he tells me. But I listen. He didn't say much about his dad of course, but his mum works on the buses in London, a "clippy", he says – that's someone who sells the tickets. That's about all I know about him so far, except that he twiddles his hair when he's upset and he doesn't like cats because they smile at him. He's a good one to talk. He's always smiling at me. If he's living with us, he'd better be nice to Tips, that's all I can say. He twiddles his hair a lot at school. I've noticed it in class, especially when he's doing his writing. He can't do his handwriting very well. Mrs Blumfeld tries to help him with his letters and his spelling but he still keeps getting everything back to front. (I think he's frightened of them – of letters, I mean.) He's good with numbers though. He doesn't have to use his fingers at all. He does it all in his head, which I can't do.

Grandfather's still telling everyone he's not going to be moved out. Lots of people have had a go at persuading him, the vicar, Doctor Morrison, even Major Tucker came to see us from the Manor House. But Grandfather won't budge. He just carries on as if nothing is happening. Half the village has moved out now, including Farmer Gent next door. I saw the last of his machinery being taken away yesterday. All his animals have gone already. They went to market last week. His farmhouse is empty. Usually I can see a light or two on in there from my window, but not any more. It's dark now, pitch black. It's like the house has gone too.

We see more and more American soldiers and lorries coming into the village every day. Grandfather's turning a blind eye to all of it. Barry's out with him now. They've gone milking. I saw them go off together a while ago, stomping across the yard in their wellies. Barry looked like he'd been doing it all his life, as if he'd always lived here, as if he was Grandfather's grandson. To tell the truth I feel a little jealous. No, that's not really true. I feel a *lot* jealous. I've often thought Grandfather wanted me to be a boy. Now I'm sure of it.

Thursday, December 16th 1943

When school ends tomorrow it'll be the end of term and that's four days earlier than we thought. We've got four days' extra holiday. Hooray! Yippee! That's because they've got to move out all the desks, the blackboard, the bookshelves, everything, down to the last piece of chalk. Mrs Blumfeld told us the American soldiers will be coming tomorrow to help us move out. We'll be going to school in Kingsbridge after Christmas. There'll be a bus to take us in because it's too far to walk. And Mrs Blumfeld said today that she'll go on being our teacher there. We all cheered and we meant it too. She's the best teacher I've ever had, only sometimes I still don't exactly understand her because of how she speaks. Because she's from Holland we've got lots of pictures of Amsterdam on the wall. They've got canals instead of roads there. She's put up two big paintings, both by Dutchmen, one of an old lady in a hat by a painter called Rembrandt (that's funny spelling, but it's right), and one of colourful ships on a beach by someone else. I can't remember his name, I think it's Van something or other. I was looking at that one today while we were practising carols. We were singing I *Saw Three Ships Come Sailing In*, and there they were up on the wall, all these ships. Funny that. I don't really understand that carol. What's three ships sailing in got to do with the birth of Jesus? I like the tune though. I'm humming it now as I write.

We all think she's very brave to go on teaching us like she has after her husband was drowned. Everyone else in the village likes her now. She's always out cycling in her blue headscarf, ringing her bell and waving whenever she sees us. I hope she doesn't remember how mean I was to her when she first came. I don't think she can do because she chose me to sing a solo in the carol concert, the first verse of *In the Bleak Midwinter*. I practise all the time: on the way home, out in the fields, in the bath. Barry says it sounds really good, which is nice of him. And he doesn't pick his nose at all any more, nor smile at me all the time. Maybe he knows he doesn't need to smile at me – maybe he knows I like him. My singing sounds really good in the bath, I know it does. But I can't take the bath into church, can I?

Saturday, December 18th 1943

I love Christmas carols, especially *In the Bleak Midwinter*. I wish we didn't only sing them at Christmas time. We had our carol concert this afternoon in the church and I had to sing my verse in front of everyone. I wobbled a bit on one or two notes, but that's because I was trembling all over, like a leaf, just before I did it. Barry told me it sounded perfect, but I knew he said that just to make me happy. And it did, but then I thought about it. The thing is that Barry can sing only on one note, so he wouldn't really know if it sounded good or bad, would he?

There's only a fortnight to go now before we're supposed to leave. Barry keeps asking me what will happen to Grandfather if he doesn't move out. He's frightened they'll take him off to prison. That's because we had a visit yesterday from the army and the police telling Grandfather he had to pack up and go, or he'd be in real trouble. Grandfather saw them off good and proper, but they said they'll be back. I just wish Barry wouldn't keep asking me about what's going to happen, because I don't know, do I? No one does. Maybe they will put him in prison. Maybe they'll put us all in prison. It makes me very frightened every time I think about it. So I'll try not to. If I do think about it, then I'll just have to make myself worry about something else.

This evening Barry and me were sitting at the top of the staircase in our dressing gowns listening to Mum and Grandfather arguing about it again down in the kitchen. Grandfather sounded more angry than I've ever heard him. He said he'd rather shoot himself than be moved off the farm. He kept on about how he doesn't hold with this war anyhow, and never did, how he went through the last one in the trenches and that was horror enough for one lifetime. "If people only knew what it was really like," he said, and he sounded as if he was almost crying he was so angry. "If they knew, if they'd seen what I've seen, they'd never send young men off to fight again. Never." He just wanted to be left alone in peace to do his farming.

Again and again Mum tried to reason with him, tried to tell him that everyone in the village was leaving, not just us; that no one wanted to go but we had to, so that the Americans could practise their landings, go over to France, and finish the war quickly. Then we'd all be back home soon enough and Dad would be back with us and the war would be over and done with. It would only be for a short time, she said. They'd promised. But Grandfather wouldn't believe her and he wouldn't believe them. He said the Yanks were just saying that so they could get him out.

In the end he slammed out of the house and left her. We heard Mum crying, so we went downstairs. Barry made her a cup of tea, and I held her hands and told her it would be all right, that I was sure Grandfather would give in and go in the end. But I was just saying it. He won't go, not of his own accord anyway, not in a million years. They'll have to carry him out, and, like Mum said, when they do it will break his heart.

Thursday, December 23rd 1943

Letter from Dad to all of us, wishing us a happy Christmas. He says he's in Italy now, and it's nothing but rain and mud and you go up one hill and there's always another one ahead of you, but that at least each hill brings him nearer home. We'd just finished reading it at breakfast when there was a knock on the door. It was Mrs Blumfeld. She was bringing her Christmas card, she said. Mum asked her in. She was all red in the face and breathless from her cycling. It seemed so strange having her here in the house. She didn't seem like our teacher at all, more like a visiting aunt. Tips was up on her lap as soon as she'd sat down. She sipped her tea and said how nice Tips was, even when she was sharpening her claws on her knees.

Then suddenly she looked across at Grandfather. I don't remember everything she said, but it was something like this. "You and me, Mr Tregenza," she said, "I think we have so much – how do you say it in English? – in common." Grandfather looked a bit flummoxed (good word that). "They tell me you are the only one in the village who won't leave. I would be just like you, I think. I loved our home in Holland, in Amsterdam. It is where I grew up. All I loved was in our home. But we had to leave; we could do nothing else. There was no choice for us because the Germans were coming. They were invading our country. We did what we could to stop them but it was no good. There were too many tanks and planes. They were too strong for us. My husband, Jacobus, was a Jew, Mr Tregenza. I am a Jew. We knew what they wanted to do with Jews. They wanted to kill us all, like rats, get rid of us. We knew this. So we had to leave our home. We came to England, Mr Tregenza, where we could be safe. Jacobus, he joined the merchant navy. He was a sea captain in Holland. We Dutch are good sailors, like you English. He was a good man and a very kind man, as you are – Barry has told me this and Lily too. They may have killed him, Mr Tregenza, but they have not killed me, not yet.

They would if they could. If they come here they will."

Grandfather's eyes never left her face all the time she was talking. "That is why I ask you to leave your home, as I did, so that the American soldiers can come. They will borrow your house and your fields for a few months to do their practising. Then they can go across the sea and liberate my people and my country, and many other countries too. This way the Germans will never come here, never march in your streets. This way my people will not suffer any longer. I know it is hard, Mr Tregenza, but I ask you to do this for me, for my husband, for my country – for your country too. I think you will, because I know you have a good heart."

I could see Grandfather's eyes were full of tears. He got up, shrugged on his coat and pulled on his hat without ever saying a word. At the door he stopped and turned around. Then all he said was, "I'll say one thing, missus. I wish I'd had a teacher like you when I was a little 'un." Then he went out and Barry ran out after him, and we were left there looking at one another in silence.

Mrs Blumfeld didn't stay long after that, and we didn't see Grandfather and Barry again until they came back for lunch. Grandfather was washing his hands in the sink when he suddenly said that he'd been thinking it over and that we could all start packing up after lunch, that he'd begin moving the sheep over to Uncle George's right away, and he'd be needing both Barry and me to give him a hand. Then very quietly he said: "Just so long as we can come back afterwards."

"We will, I promise," Mum told him, and she went over to hug him. He cried then. That was the first time I've ever seen Grandfather cry.

Saturday, December 25th 1943

Christmas Day. There's no point in pretending this was a happy Christmas. We tried to make the best of it. We had decorations everywhere as usual and a nice Christmas tree. We had our stockings all together in Grandfather's bed. But Dad wasn't there. Mum missed him a lot and so did I. Barry was homesick too and Grandfather was really down in the dumps all day and grumpy about moving. We had roast chicken for lunch, which did make everyone feel a little happier. I found a silver threepenny bit in the Christmas pudding and Barry found one too, so that made him forget he was homesick, for a while anyway. We all gave Grandfather a hand with the evening milking to cheer him up, and it worked, but not for long. There's only a week to go now before we have to have everything out of here. It's all Grandfather can think about. The house is piled high with tea chests and boxes. The curtains and lamp shades are all down, most of the crockery is already packed. We may have the Christmas decorations up, but it doesn't feel at all like Christmas.

For my present I got a pair of red woolly gloves that Mum had knitted specially and secretly, and Barry had a navy blue scarf which he wears all the time, even at meal times. Mum didn't knit that, she didn't have time. We all went off to church this evening. It's the last time we'll be doing that for a long while. They're going to empty it of all its precious things – stained glass windows, candlesticks, benches – in case they get damaged. The American soldiers are coming to take it all away. They'll be putting sandbags around everything that's too heavy to move, so that everything will be protected as much as possible. That's what the vicar told us – he also said they'll be needing all the help they can get. They're starting to empty the church tomorrow. Mum says we've all got to be there to lend a hand.

I gave Tips some cold chicken this evening for her Christmas supper. She licked the plate until it was shiny clean. She's a bit upset, I think. She knows something's up. She can see it for herself and she can feel it too. I think she's unhappy because she knows we're unhappy.

I'm getting a bit fed up with Uncle George already, and we haven't even moved in with him yet. All he talks about is the war: the Germans this and the Russians that. He sits there with his ear practically glued to the radio, tutting and huffing at the news. Even today, on Christmas Day, he has to go on and on about how we should "bomb Germany to smithereens, because of all they've done to us"! Then once he got talking about it, everyone was talking about it, arguing about it. So I came up to bed and left them to it. It's supposed to be a day of peace and goodwill towards all men. And all they can talk about is the war. It makes me so sad, and I shouldn't be sad on Christmas Day. But now I am. Happy Christmas, Dad.

PS Just after I finished my diary I heard Barry crying in his room, so I went to see him. He didn't want to tell me at first. Then he said he was just a bit homesick, missing his mum, he said. And his dad – mostly his dad. What could I say? My dad is alive and I'm living in my own home, going to my own school. Then I had an idea. "Shall we say Happy Christmas to the cows?" I said. He cheered up at once. So we crept downstairs in our dressing gowns and slippers, and ran out to the barn. They were all lying down in the straw grunting and chewing the cud, their calves curled up asleep beside them. Barry crouched down and stroked one

of them, who sucked his finger until he giggled and pulled it out. We were walking back across the yard when he told me. "I hate the radio," he said suddenly. "It's always about the war, and the bombing raids, and that's when I think of Mum most and miss her most. I don't want her to die. I don't want to be an orphan."

I held his hand and squeezed it. I was too upset to say anything.

Sunday, December 26th 1943

I've had the strangest day and the happiest day for a long time. I met someone who's the most different person I've ever met. He's different in every way. He looks different, he sounds different, he is different. And, best of all, he's my friend.

We were supposed to be helping to move things out of the church, but mostly we were just watching, because the Yanks were doing it all for us. Grandfather's right: they do chew gum a lot. But they're very happy-looking, always laughing and joking around. Some of them were carrying sandbags into the church, whilst others were carrying out the pews and chairs, hymn books and kneelers.

Suddenly I recognised one of them. He was the same black soldier I had seen in the jeep a while ago. And he recognised me too. "Hi there! How you doing?" he said. I never saw anyone smile like he did. His whole face lit up with it. He looked too young to be a soldier. He seemed so pleased to see me there, someone he recognised. He bent down so that his face was very close to mine. "I got three little sisters back home in Atlanta – that's in Georgia and that's in the United States of America, way across the sea," he said. "And they's all pretty, just like you."

Then another soldier came along – I think he was a sergeant or something because he had lots of stripes on his arm, upside-down ones, not like our soldiers' stripes at all. The sergeant told him he should be carrying sandbags, not chatting to kids. So he said, "Yessir." Then he went off, smiling back at me over his shoulder. The next time I saw him he was coming past me with a sandbag under each arm. He stopped right by me and looked down at me from very high up. "What do you call yourself, girl?" he asked me. So I told him. Then he said, "I'm Adolphus T. Madison. (That's T for Thomas.) Private First Class, US Army. My friends call me Adie. I'm mighty pleased to make your acquaintance, Lily. A ray of Atlanta sunshine, that's

what you are, a ray of Atlanta sunshine."

No one has ever talked to me like that before. He looked me full in the eye as he spoke, so I knew he meant every word he said. But the sergeant shouted at him again and he had to go.

Then Barry came along, and for the rest of the morning we stood at the back of the church watching the soldiers coming and going, all of them fetching and carrying sandbags now, and Adie would give me a great big grin every time he went by. The vicar was fussing about them like an old hen, telling the Yank soldiers they had to be more careful, particularly when they were sandbagging the font. "That font's very precious, you know," said the vicar. I could see they didn't like being pestered, but they were all too polite and respectful to say anything. The vicar kept on and on nagging at them. "It's the most precious thing in the church. It's Norman, you know, very old." A couple of Yanks were just coming past us with more sandbags a few moments later when one of them said, "Who is this old Norman guy, anyway?"

After that Barry and me couldn't stop ourselves giggling. The vicar told us we shouldn't be giggling in church, so we went outside and giggled in the graveyard instead.

We told Grandfather and Mum about that when

we got back this evening and they laughed so much they nearly cried. It's been a happy, happy day. I hope Adie doesn't get killed in the war. He's so nice. I'm going to pray for him tonight, and for Dad too.

Tips has just brought in a dead mouse and dropped it at my feet. She knows how much I hate mice, dead or alive. I really wish she wouldn't do it. She's sitting there, licking her lips and looking so pleased with herself. Sometimes I think I understand why Barry doesn't like cats.

Monday, December 27th 1943

It's my very last night in my own bedroom. Until now I don't think I thought it would ever really happen, not to us, not to me. It was happening to everyone else. Everyone else was moving out, but somehow I just didn't imagine that the day would ever come when we'd have to do the same. But tomorrow is the final day and tomorrow will come. This time tomorrow my room will be empty – the whole house will be empty. I've never slept anywhere else in my whole life except in this room. For the first time I think I understand why Grandfather refused to leave for so long. It wasn't just because he was being stubborn and difficult and grumpy. He loves this place, and so do I. I look around this room and it's a part of me. I belong here. I'll start to cry if I write any more, so I'll stop.

Tuesday, December 28th 1943

Our first night at Uncle George's and it's cold. But there's something worse than that, much worse. Tips has gone missing. We haven't got her with us.

We moved up here today. We were the last ones in the whole village to move out. Grandfather is very proud of that. We had lots of help. Mrs Blumfeld came and so did Adie, along with half a dozen other Yanks. We couldn't have managed without them. Everything is here, all the tea chests, all the furniture. Most of it is stored in Uncle George's granary under an old tarpaulin. But the cows are still back home on the farm. We'll go back for them tomorrow, Grandfather said, and drive them up the lane.

Uncle George has made room here for all of us. He's very kind, I suppose, but he talks to himself too much and he grunts and wheezes a lot, and when he blows his nose it sounds like a foghorn.

He's very dirty and scruffy and untidy, which Mum doesn't like, and I think he's a bit proud too. I was only trying to be polite, because Mum said I should be, when I asked him which chair was his before I sat down. Uncle George said: "They'm all my chairs Lil." (I wish he wouldn't call me Lil, only Mum and Dad call me that.) He was laughing as he said it, but he meant it, I know he did. I think it's because he's Mum's eldest brother that he's a bit bossy with us. He keeps saying Dad shouldn't have gone off to the war and left her on her own. That's what I think too, but I don't like it when Uncle George says it. Anyway, she's not on her own. She's got Grandfather and she's got me.

Mum says I have to be very patient with him because he's a bachelor, which means that he's lived on his own all his life which is why he's untidy and doesn't know how to get on with people very well. I'll try, but it's not going to be easy. And what's more, he looks like a scarecrow, except when he's in his Home Guard uniform.

When he's in his uniform he looks very pleased with himself. Grandfather says he doesn't do much in the Home Guard, that he just sits up in the lookout post on top of the hill. They're supposed to be looking for enemy ships and planes, but Grandfather says they just have a good natter and a smoke.

I miss my room at home already. My bedroom here is not just cold, it's very small, a bit like a cupboard – a cupboard I have to share with Mum. Barry's in with Grandfather. It was the only way to fit us all in. Mum and me have to share a bed too, but I don't mind that. We'll cuddle up. She'll keep me warm! I haven't got a table, so I'm writing this sitting up in bed with my diary on my knees.

I wish Tips was here. I miss her and I'm really worried about her. She ran off when everyone came to the house to carry the furniture out. I called and called, but she didn't come. I'm trying my best not to be worried. Mum says she's just gone off on her wanders somewhere, that she'll come back when the house is quiet again. She's sure she'll be there when we go to fetch the animals tomorrow. She keeps saying there are still three days to go before they close the farm off, but I can't stop thinking that after that we won't be allowed back for six months or even more. What if Tips isn't there tomorrow? What if we can't find her?

Barry's happier than ever, because he's got two farmers to work with now, and two tractors. But what's more surprising is that Grandfather is happy too. I thought he was going to be very sad when we left home. I was there when he locked the door and slipped the key into his waistcoat pocket. He stood looking up at the house for some moments. He even tried to smile. But he never said anything. He just took my hand and Barry's, and we all walked off without looking back. He made himself at home in Uncle George's kitchen right away. He's got his feet in the oven already, which you can see Uncle George doesn't like. But Grandfather's much older than he is, so Uncle George will just have to put up with it, won't he?

Oh yes, I forgot. This afternoon Adie introduced me to his friend Harry, while they were carrying out our kitchen table. He's from Atlanta too, and he's black like Adie is. They're both quite difficult to understand sometimes because they speak English differently from us. Adie does most of the talking. "Harry's like my brother, Lily, not my brother brother, if you get my meaning, just my friend. Like twins, ain't we, Harry? Always on the lookout for one another. Harry and me, we growed up together, same street, same town. We was born on the same day too – 25th November. Both of us is eighteen, but I'm the oldest by six hours – that's what our mamas told us, and they should know I reckon. Ain't that right Harry?" Harry just smiled at me and nodded. "Harry don't say much," Adie said, "but he thinks real deep." The two of them worked together all day, fetching and carrying. They must be very strong too. They picked up Grandfather's dresser all by themselves. No huffing, no puffing.

They just picked it up as if it was light as a feather.

I keep thinking I hear Tips outside, but every time I look it's Uncle George's ginger tomcat mewing round the yard. I just hope Tips gets on with Uncle George's cat. Tips doesn't much like other cats. But if I've got to be polite to Uncle George, then she'll have to be polite to Uncle George's cat, won't she? This time tomorrow Tips will be here and everything will be just tickety-boo! That word always makes me smile, even when I'm sad. So I'll write it again: tickety-boo, tickety-boo. The lamp's just gone out so I suppose I'll have to finish now.

Thursday, December 30th 1943

I still can't find Tips. I've been looking for her all day today – and all yesterday too. I looked in every barn, every shed. Grandfather opened up the house again for me and I went into every room, up into the attic too. I looked in all the cupboards, just in case she'd got herself shut in by mistake. Grandfather even climbed up a ladder to look in the roof valleys. I wandered the fields, tapping her bowl with a spoon, calling and calling, then listening for her. All I could hear were cawing crows and the sound of the wind in the trees and the rumble of a tractor engine in the distance. Once they'd driven the cows and sheep up the lane to Uncle George's everyone came back to help me. Mrs Blumfeld went off to search the village on her bike, with Barry on the back. They didn't find Tips, but they did find lots of Yanks. They were all over the place, they said, in lorries and jeeps and some of them in tanks.

Mum still says I'm not to worry. Grandfather says that cats have nine lives, that Tips will turn up as she always does, and it's true she always has. But I do worry. I can't think about anything else now except Tips. She's out there somewhere in the night, cold and wet, hungry and lost, and I've only got one more day to find her before they close off the farm. I'm going to get up early tomorrow; Barry says he'll come with me. We're going to look and look until we find her, he says. I'm not coming back to Uncle George's until I do.

Our farm looked strange when I went back today, so empty and silent: a phantom farm, a house full of ghosts.

Be there tomorrow, Tips. Please be there. It's your last chance.

Friday, December 31st 1943

I never want to live another day like this. I think I knew right from the start we wouldn't find her. There were too many people out looking – I knew they would only frighten her away, and they did. If it had just been Barry and me and Mum and Grandfather, maybe we'd have found her. Tips knows us.

It wasn't her fault. Mrs Blumfeld was only trying to be helpful, but she'd gone and told everyone how Tips was lost and she brought practically the whole village along with her. She was there at dawn organising the search. The Yanks came too, dozens of them, Adie and Harry telling them all the places they had to look. They combed the whole farm: every barn, every feed bin, every corner of every field, all along the stream. They went searching down in the bluebell wood, down in the disused quarry, and I went with them, trying to tell them all the time to go more quietly, just to look, not call out. But it was no use. I could hear them all over the farm, banging tins, trying to call her, trying to sweeten Tips in.

All morning long it drizzled and in the afternoon a sea mist came rolling in over the fields and covered the whole farm in thick fog, so you couldn't see further than a few feet in front of you. There was no point in even looking any more. We listened instead, but there was nothing to hear. Even the crows were silent. I think I've been crying off and on all day, as the hours passed and hope faded. Barry kept on and on telling me he was sure we'd find her sooner or later and in the end I got cross and shouted at him, which I shouldn't have done. He was only trying to cheer me up, trying to be nice. That's the trouble with him, he's always trying to be nice. Uncle George just said that a cat's a cat, that there're other cats I can have, which didn't exactly help.

It was nearly dark when one of the Yanks with upside-down stripes on his arm said he was sorry but they had orders to close the place off now, so we had to leave. Adie came up and gave me some chocolate. "Hershey bar," he said. "It'll make you feel better. And don't you worry none, Lily. I ain't making no promises, but if that old cat's still living out there, we're gonna find her, one way or the other. You can be real sure of that. So don't you worry none, Lily, y'hear."

They closed the barbed wire behind us then, cutting us off from our home and from Tips. I promised myself as I watched them that I would go back and find her, and I will too. I will. I gave

Barry half my Hershey Bar to make up for being so mean to him, and we ate it before we got back to Uncle George's. Adie was right. It did make me feel better, but I think that was more because I gave half of it to Barry.

I'm coughing a lot and I'm feeling hot and sweaty all over. I have been ever since we got back. Mum says I've caught a chill and that I have to stay in bed tomorrow else it'll get on my chest. I hated today, every horrible minute of it – except for Adie and the Hershey bar. The only hope I've got left is that maybe, just maybe, Adie and Harry might still find Tips. I've got this feeling they might. I don't know why. One thing's for sure though: if they don't find her then I'm going to crawl in under the wire and find her for myself, no matter what they say. They can put up all the barbed wire they like. They can shoot all the shells they want. Nothing's going to keep me out. I'm never ever going to give up on Tips. Never.

Wednesday, January 12th 1944

This is the first time I've felt like writing in my diary for days. Mum was right, I did catch a chill that day when we all went out looking for Tips, and it did go to my chest. Mum told me I had a temperature of 104 for nearly a week and the doctor had to be called because I became delirious. That sounds like it means I was just happy – I certainly was not. It meant I was out of my head. And I must have been because I remember very little. I only remember bits of the last few days. I remember Barry coming in after school and telling me what the new school in Kingsbridge was like and giving me get-well cards from Mrs Blumfeld and the class. I remember waking up to see Grandfather and Mum sitting in the chair watching me, or just sitting there sleeping. And from time to time I could hear the murmur of voices downstairs and Uncle George blowing his nose like a foghorn.

I'm much better now, but Mum says I've got to

stay inside for at least another week. Doctor's orders, she says, but I think they're just *her* orders. She always gets very fierce and strict with me when I'm ill. She's been feeding me soup and then sitting and watching me, just to make sure I finish it. She makes me eat stewed apple every day and I have to drink lots of warm milk with honey in it. She knows I hate milk. But now she's got the perfect excuse to make me drink it. "It'll build up your strength, Lily," she says. "Drink it." And she always stays until I do.

As for Tips, there's still no sign of her. No one has been back to look for her, of course. But I haven't given up. I still keep hoping she's all right, that one day she'll come and find us. She's a good hunter, she can take care of herself. She knows warm places to go. I try to hope and believe Adie will find her somehow. But then when I think about it again I know he won't. I keep thinking of her lying dead in some ditch. I try not to think like that. I try so hard. Soon as I'm better, I'm going to go looking for her. I promised myself I would, and I will.

Mum came up today and read me a letter from Dad. It's such a long time since I saw him I find it difficult to see his face in my head any more. I tried to hear his voice as she was reading the letter, but I couldn't. He says they had corned beef and tinned potatoes for Christmas lunch, and they wore paper hats made out of newspaper, sang Christmas carols and thought of home. He sounded so sad and far away. When Mum finished reading she was sad too. I could tell she wanted to cry but she wouldn't let herself.

Wednesday, January 19th 1944

I've been planning it for days, working it all out and screwing up my courage to do it. And today I did it. But it didn't work out at all like I had planned.

I'm getting really good at telling lies. I told Mum I just wanted to go out for some fresh air, that I was fed up with being cooped up. I nagged and nagged and finally Mum gave in, but only because it was a nice, sunshiney day, she said. She wrapped me up as if I was going out into the Arctic – gloves, hat, scarf, coat, the lot – and she told me to keep out of the wind, and I had to promise her I'd be back inside an hour. I promised... with my fingers crossed.

It wasn't that difficult to get through the wire. There was no one about to see me. I just wriggled my way through and made off across the field towards home, keeping behind the hedges so that I was always out of sight of Uncle George's house.

Home looked so empty and deserted when I got there: no hens scratching anywhere, no geese on the pond. I called for Tips as loudly as I dared. I looked in all the places I thought she might be hiding: the granary, the shippen, the milking parlour, the piggery. Then I remembered that one of Tips's favourite sleeping places was always up in the hay barn. I walked through the abandoned farmyard and was just climbing up the ladder into the hay loft when I heard voices outside the barn. It sounded like there were two of them, and they were American. That was when I felt a sneeze coming on, and there was nothing I could do to stop it. I couldn't help myself. I don't think I've ever sneezed so loudly in all my life.

I couldn't think what else to do. I lay down in the hay loft and pulled the hay over me so I was completely covered and tried to stop myself breathing. I heard them coming into the barn, heard them as they came up the ladder.

Then there was silence for a few moments. I was thinking I might just have got away with it, when suddenly I was grabbed by my wellies and yanked out. There were Adie and Harry staring down at me.

"Lily! Well, I'll be damned!" Adie said pushing back his helmet. "Look what we got ourselves here, Harry. Now, if I ain't mistook, Lily, you come looking for your cat, that right?" I nodded. "What you wanna do that for? Didn't I tell you we'd find her? Didn't I? Didn't I? Ain't you got no faith?" His whole face suddenly became very serious. "You got to promise me something," he said. "You got to promise you won't never come near this place again. You do what I say, Lily, or you gonna get yourself in real trouble. You gonna get yourself hurt bad, real bad, you hear me? Ain't worth it, not for no cat it ain't. Soon enough this here's gonna be a mighty dangerous place to be. You gotta stay outa here. You promise me, now." He was really angry with me. So I promised. They helped me down the ladder and together we ran through the farmyard, past the farmhouse and out over the fields to the perimeter wire, Adie holding my hand the whole way. I squeezed through. "Don't you never come inside the wire again." Adie said. "You just stay where you is, Lily. And don't you go worrying yourself. We'll find that old cat for you, and that's a faithful promise, ain't it, Harry?"

"Faithful promise," said Harry.

Then they walked away and I watched them go until I couldn't see them any more.

Mum met me at the door. She had her coat on. She was just coming out to look for me. "Look at the state of you," she said, and began brushing all the hay off my coat. "Where've you been?"

"In the barn," I told her. And that wasn't a lie, was it?

I've had such a supreme day, even though I didn't find Tips. I should be sad, but I'm not. I keep living it all again and again in my head, every exciting moment of it. I shan't sleep tonight. I know I shan't.

Monday, January 24th 1944

Back at school. Everyone else had been back for a long time of course and so they all knew each other and I didn't. All my friends from the village school already had lots of new friends from Kingsbridge School who I'd never seen before, and no one seemed that pleased to see me. I would have felt a bit out of it if Barry hadn't stuck by me like he did. He showed me round too, showed me where to line up, where to hang my coat. It felt a bit strange, a townie showing me round. But I don't think of Barry as a townie any more, not really. He kept telling everyone about Tips, and about how I'd been ill, so as a result everyone was very nice to me in the end. I'm going to make a promise to myself. From now on I'm never to be nasty to Barry again, even when I get irritated. He was really kind today. In playtime someone mistook him for my brother and I didn't mind at all. In fact I quite liked it, so I didn't say he wasn't.

I'm in Mrs Blumfeld's class which is supreme. We had a lesson about America, about all the states which are the stars on the flag, and she told us they've got a president instead of a king. She says it's this huge place, miles bigger than England, with great big lakes as big as England, with great high mountains called the Rockies, and they've got prairies and deserts, and canyons too. She didn't say what canyons were. She told us they play baseball not cricket, and how lots of different kinds of people live there from all over the world, how they all went there to find a place to live, to find freedom and to make a new kind of country, and how now they've come all the way back across the Atlantic to help us win the war against Hitler. I'd like to go there one day. I'm going to ask Adie more about it when I see him again. I'll ask him what a canyon is too.

At tea time Uncle George came in stamping his boots and told us it was snowing really hard outside. It was too. The sky was full of great heavy flakes that landed on my face and made me close my eyes when I looked up. I caught them on my tongue and let them melt. Then I thought of Tips out there in the cold and the dark and I started crying – I couldn't help myself. I called and called for her until Mum heard me and fetched me in. She was angry with me for going out, until she saw I'd been crying, then she was nice again. She put me in a hot bath to warm me through which was lovely, and made me drink a glass of hot milk with honey, which was not lovely at all. It was dis-gust-ing. Why can't cows make something nice instead? Like lemonade for instance.

I've thought of something. If the snow keeps falling like it is, if it doesn't melt, then there'll be footprints, won't there? Maybe tomorrow I could find Tips's paw prints and if I did, I could follow them and find her.

PS I've just woken up. Mum's got up and gone milking already. I'm looking out of the window as I write. It's early morning and still quite dark, only it's white all around because of the snow. It looks new and fresh, like the world's just been made. I can see Mum walking towards the milking parlour, leaving her footprints behind her across the farmyard. She's blowing on her hands; I can see her breath in the air. I've thought of something else: if Tips leaves her prints in the snow then I'll leave mine, won't I? And if I leave mine then someone could find them going through the wire and follow me. No good. I'll have to think of some other way. Back to sleep. I'm tired.

PPS I've woken up again. I just had this dream about Tips, and what's more it was a dream that came true in a way. I want to write it down now before I forget it. I dreamt she came looking for us through the snow, that she found her way in through the kitchen window, ran up the stairs, pushed open the door and jumped on the bed, and was purring in my ear. When I woke up just now I was so happy because my dream had come true. I could feel her warmth against my face. She was back, she was purring in my ear! But then I woke up properly, and it wasn't her at all. It was Uncle George's tomcat. He's still here and he's looking up at me out of his wide yellow eyes. I wish they were Tips's eyes. Uncle George's cat wants me to love him. But I can't.

Maybe Tips isn't ever going to come back. For the first time I'm beginning to think that perhaps she has gone for ever. I mustn't think like that. I mustn't. Once the snow's gone I'm going to go and look again and again until I find her. She's got to be alive, she's just got to be. If she is alive she'll be looking for food, won't she?

Stupid! Stupid! Why didn't I think of it before? I'll pinch some food from the larder, leftovers. No one will notice, not if I don't take much, not if I'm careful. I'll put it out for her in the hay barn back home. Then I'll watch and wait for her. She'll be hungry. She'll come. She's got to come. She must.

Thursday, February 10th 1944

I must have been in and out through the wire looking for Tips half a dozen times or more now. Every time the food I'd put out for her was gone, but I was never there when she came for it. I was so sure that sooner or later I'd get lucky, and she'd come while I was there, while I was waiting for her.

Then today the very worst happened. I went off as usual after tea, when everyone else was feeding up the animals. No one was about. As usual the food I put out in the hay barn yesterday had gone. So I put down some more and then waited up in the hay loft, hoping and hoping this time she'd come while I was there. That was when the dog came running into the barn, a huge Alsatian, as big as a wolf. He went straight to the food and snuffled it up. He knew exactly where it was. It was him! It was the dog who'd been taking it all along. Maybe I moved. Maybe he smelt me. I don't know.

All I know is that he looked up and began barking at me, teeth bared, his hackles up, his whole body shaking.

Then there were sounds of voices and running feet, and the American soldiers came. They were looking up at me and pointing their rifles and shouting at me to come down. They couldn't see me, but they knew I was up there all right. They kept shouting and saying they were going to shoot unless I came down. So I did. I was hoping Adie would be there, or Harry, but it wasn't them. All their faces were white. The dog looked as if it was going to eat me, so I waited halfway up the ladder till they caught him and held him. One of them said, "Holy cow! It's a kid!" And then they walked me outside and bundled me into the back of a jeep. I kept telling them I was a friend of Adie's, but that didn't seem to make them any kinder towards me. They weren't rough with me, but they weren't exactly nice to me either. They said they were taking me to see the captain, that I was in real trouble.

The next thing I knew I was being marched into this room and there was this captain with a bald head, sitting behind a desk, looking up at me and asking me all sorts of questions, like what my name was, what I was doing there, and where did I live. So I told him and he shook his head and said didn't I know I could have got myself killed. I said no. Then he got angry at me, banged the table and told me I was never, never to go through the wire again, and did I understand. I said I did, but I just wanted to find Tips. And he said who was Tips and I said she was my cat. Then he said, "Jesus Christ Almighty," which he shouldn't have said, because you're not supposed to say things like that, unless you're praying, that is. Then he bawled out a command of some kind and in came another soldier and saluted. It was Adie. Was I glad to see him! "They say you know this kid, Soldier. That right?" the captain asked.

"Yessir," said Adie, standing very stiffly beside me and not looking at all pleased to see me. "She was just playing around, Captain, like kids do. She didn't mean no harm by it." Adie was told to take me home, to tell my mother and make sure it didn't happen again. "Yessir, Captain," said Adie and saluted again.

I smiled up at Adie as he took me out, to thank him for coming to my rescue. He didn't smile back at all. He walked me silently to the jeep and drove me all the way back home without a single word. He turned off the engine by the farm gate, out of sight of the house. "You're some crazy girl, you know that?" he said. He lit up a cigarette, and his face glowed in the dark and I could see now that he was really angry with me. "Here's what I'm gonna do, Lily," he said. "I'm not gonna tell your mama about what you done, if you promise me you won't do this no more. But you gotta promise like you mean it."

"I promise," I told him, but I didn't mean it.

"Now you listen to me real good. I been looking, Harry's been looking. We're gonna find that cat for you. Didn't I tell you? Didn't I say? But if you goes snooping about, I'm telling you, either you gonna get yourself blowed to bits, or they gonna catch you again. I'm serious here. We got patrols in there all day, every day. They'll catch you, Lily. Ain't no way they won't. Ain't no way I can save your hide next time." He told me I could go, so I got out of the jeep. He looked at me for a moment as I stood there and shook his head. "Just like my little sisters you is. Trouble. Nothin' but trouble. And stubborn as a mule. I knowed you were trouble moment I first saw you. You do what Adie says now. You be good, you hear." Then he drove off and left me there.

I think Adie knows I'm not going to be good. He knows I'm going back in to look for Tips. And I am too, because now I know for sure what's been stopping Tips from coming out of hiding and eating my food. That American guard dog, that Alsatian. I know what I'm going to do. I'm going to wake up early; I'll wait till Mum goes off to do the milking. No one will see me, will they? It'll still be dark in the early morning, so I should be safe enough if I don't take too long. And Tips always likes going out hunting when it's dark. She's probably hiding up somewhere by day, scared stiff of that guard dog. Don't blame her. That's probably why I haven't been able to find her all this time. But I'll find her now. She'll come out in the dark, I know she will. I'll find you Tips, I promise – I will.

I so want to tell someone everything that happened to me today. I think Barry's the only person I could tell. No one else would believe me. Maybe I'll tell him tomorrow.

Friday, February 11th 1944

I don't need to tell Barry. He already knows. Here's how.

I got up early this morning, while it was still dark, just as I'd planned. There was no one about. I heard the cows mooing in the parlour as I ran across the farmyard, and I could hear Mum singing to them. She likes to sing to them when she's milking. She thinks it makes them happy, and she likes them happy because they give more milk. I scrambled through the wire in my usual place, out of sight of the farmhouse, and ran across the fields. After a while I stopped to catch my breath and to call out for Tips, and to listen. That was when I heard the sound of panting coming from behind me. I thought it was that guard dog again, coming at me out of the darkness, coming fast, and I went numb all over with fear. But it wasn't the dog that came out of the darkness. It was Barry and he was angry at me, angry like I'd never seen him. He got hold of me and was shaking me. He said he knew I'd been up to something. He'd got up to go milking with Mum and he'd seen me running off. He was shrieking at me. "What do you think you're doing, Lily? It's dangerous. You shouldn't be here. It's going to be a battlefield. Live ammunition, Lily – shells, bombs, bullets. There's signs up everywhere. DANGER – LIVE FIRING. Can't you read? You're not allowed!" Then he stopped his shouting and suddenly let me go. "You've been in here before! You've been through the wire lots of times, haven't you?" he said. "You're looking for Tips, aren't you?"

When I began to cry he sat me down under the hedge. I told him everything then, all about Adie and Harry, all about yesterday, and how I'd looked and looked and couldn't find Tips anywhere, how I was sure she was still alive. Barry didn't say anything for a while, just picked at the grass. "You won't tell, will you?" I said.

"'Course not," he replied. "What do you think I am? But we've got to get out of here. Now!"

"Just one more look," I said. "Please, Barry. She could be waiting for us right now. Please." I knew he'd let me and he did.

As we walked across the fields together, the moon seemed to be floating on the sea. There were lots of ships in the bay, more than usual. In spite of the moonlight the sky was darker out there over the sea than over the hills beyond the farm. Dawn was breaking there. No sun yet, only the grey beginning of a new day. All was quiet. We climbed the gate and stood there, just listening. We began to call for her, softly at first, then a little louder, then as loud as we dared. There was no answering call, only an empty, eerie silence. But it was strange, because I felt the silence seemed to be waiting for something to happen, so when it did I wasn't nearly as surprised as I should have been.

Suddenly the sky was filled with bright orange and yellow flashes all along the horizon and then there came a great roaring followed by huge explosions, one after the other: down on the beach, in the village, explosions that were coming closer and closer to us all the time. I could feel the ground shaking under my feet. Barry took my hand and we ran, ran for our lives. But however hard we ran, the explosions seemed to be catching us up. I was screaming and screaming. I tripped and rolled over and over, and Barry fell half on top of me. Then the shelling stopped and we dared to stand up and look. In the thin light I could see there were landing craft coming through the smoke towards the beach, two or three at first, then dozens of them, the soldiers leaping out of the water and charging up the beach, firing as they came.

Barry pulled me to my feet and we ran. It seemed like miles that we ran, but we didn't stop till we reached the wire. I was in such a hurry I snagged my coat as I wriggled through and Barry had to stop and unhook me. As we walked home together, I was shaking and speechless and breathless. At the back door, before we went in, Barry made me promise never again to go through the wire. I promised, and this time I meant it.

I really meant it. I was frightened out of my skin. I'm not going back in there, not any more, not for Tips, not for all the tea in China.

All day at school Barry and I kept looking at one another. Everyone was talking about the fireworks out at sea that morning. Everyone had heard it, or heard about it, but we'd *been* there. Mrs Blumfeld said she thought it was likely to happen again and again. "They have to practise." she told us. "It's like anything, children. If you want to do something well, you have to practise. And if we want them to win the war, if we do want Europe to be free again, then we want them to practise all they want, don't we?"

Uncle George's cat is back on our bed. He thinks he's taking Tips's place. Maybe he is, but only on my bed, never in my heart.

Thursday, February 24th 1944

Mrs Blumfeld was right. The Yanks are practising almost every day now. Most days now you can hear the whoosh and thump and crump of the bombs in the distance. I was coming up the lane with Barry after school today when we heard it again. It wasn't close enough to make the earth shake, not like before. But we were close enough to hear the cracking and spitting of rifle fire, and Barry said it sounded more like they were machine guns because they were firing so fast. It sounded to me like a whole orchestra of war. It was far away but it was still frightening, and the strange thing was the birds were joining in too. It doesn't seem to frighten them at all.

Friday, March 3rd 1944

It's like a miracle. We were just sitting in the kitchen having our tea when we heard a car outside. Uncle George's dog was going mad. Mum said to see who it was. By the time we went out Uncle George's dog was attacking the tyres, biting and snapping at them. It was a jeep. Adie was in it and Harry too. It was the first time I'd ever seen them without their helmets on. They looked even younger somehow, not men at all like the other soldiers. More like boys. "Got something for you, Lily," said Adie, and his smile seemed like a laugh waiting to happen. "Something that's gonna make you real happy."

I thought it would be some chocolate or something. But it wasn't. Harry reached into the back of the jeep and lifted out a cardboard box – a cardboard box which was mewing! "You said black and white, right?" Harry said, giving it to me. "We found this one hiding away in that old hotel down on the beach. She's blacker'n me and whiter'n you. Scratches some too."

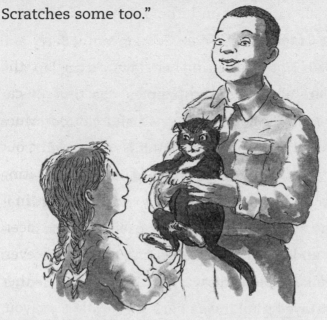

Adie took her and held her out to me. "This the one you been looking for?" I knew her at once, from her green eyes, from her markings, her white paws, and from the deep roaring purr inside her as I took her into my arms and hugged her to my cheek.

I'm not sure how it all happened after that. I know I was crying a lot, then hugging Adie and Harry. I know they were about to get back in the jeep when Mum came out, and minutes later we were all sitting round the kitchen table, Adie, Harry, Grandfather, Uncle George, Mum, Barry and me with Tips sharpening her claws on my lap, and we were all having the happiest tea time of our lives. Mum got out the scones and clotted cream she had been saving for Sunday. Adie and Harry had never had scones before. Barry got some cream on his nose and tried to lick it off with his tongue and he couldn't, so he used the back of his hand and licked it and everyone laughed. And no one talked about the war, not even Uncle George. They stayed until it was dark.

I walked with Adie out to the jeep, Tips riding on my shoulder and clinging to me as if she would never let go. "Lily," he said quietly, "I gotta tell you there was other cats, young ones, a whole family of them down in that old hotel place. From the looks of her and the looks of them, I reckon they was her family, maybe too old to need mothering, but you'd better keep a good eye on her, else she could go right back to them, y'understand me?

She's here now. You keep her here." He stopped by the jeep and stroked Tips on the head. "I've had the best time, Lily, the best time since I left home," he said.

Then I asked him, "When you go out in those boats and do those landings, is it dangerous?"

He didn't answer for a moment. "They fire real live stuff over our heads, so I guess it is. But they do it so we can get used to it. They know what they're doing, I reckon. It'll be a whole lot hotter when we do it for real over in France, that's for sure."

"When will you go?" I asked him.

"Sooner the better," Adie said. "It's what we came over here for, Lily, so I just want to get on with it, get it done and get back home." Then he and Harry were gone. I realised too late that I never even said thank you.

Grandfather was sitting with his feet in the oven this evening when he turned to me and said, "Lily, I never thought I'd hear myself say it, but those gum-chewing Yanks are all right. They're all right."

Uncle George's cat hasn't been seen since Tips arrived. Tips is queen here now. She's taken over the whole house – and my bed. She's lying spread out on my feet, right now, flexing her claws and looking at me as I'm writing. She never takes her eyes off me. And Adie was right, she has had more kittens. It was some time ago but I can still tell. I just hope her kittens are old enough to do without her. I can't let her go back to them, I just can't. It's so good to have her back. I feel like I'm purring inside, purring with happiness.

I've been thinking. Next time I see Adie I'm going to ask him to bring her kittens home as well. Then Tips will be really happy like me. And she won't ever want to go running off to find them, will she?

Tuesday, March 7th 1944

Tips has gone off again. It was Barry's fault. He left the back door ajar when he went to fetch the logs. I told him. I told everyone she might make a run for it, that we had to be sure to keep her in. Tips must have slipped out behind his back and we haven't been able to find her since. Barry says he was only gone for a few moments. I try not to blame him, but in my heart I do. He should have been more careful.

I'm more cross than upset. At least I know where she must have gone: back to her kittens, back to the hotel. At least I know she's alive. As soon as I can I'll tell Adie, and he can go and fetch her back again, and the kittens too this time. He'll do it for me, I know he will.

Today was such a beautiful day too, clear skies and a blue, blue sea. There are primroses all under the hedges and celandine too. Why do sad things have to happen on beautiful days? And Barry's miserable too because he thinks I am angry with him. I'm not really, not much anyway. I'll make it up to him tomorrow. We heard lots more big explosions today – one huge one that shook the whole house. I hope Adie and Harry are all right.

Wednesday, March 8th 1944

Someone said it first on the school bus this morning. I couldn't believe it. I didn't want to believe it, but Mrs Blumfeld told us it was true. The Slapton Beach Hotel was blown up yesterday, blown to pieces during a landing exercise. She says there's nothing left but rubble. Barry picked some primroses for me on the way home this afternoon, because he thought they'd make me feel better, I suppose. But they don't. This time I know I won't see Tips again. There's no point in even hoping, not any more. She had her nine lives, I suppose, but her kittens didn't, did they? I can't even cry. I'm too sad. Uncle George's cat came in a few minutes ago. Maybe he knows what's happened, and he's trying to be kind. I've put him out now. I don't want any other cat, not ever.

Wednesday, March 15th 1944

Mum said this morning that she had a big surprise for me. I thought she was just trying to cheer me up. First she said Barry and I could stay away from school today, so we knew something was up. Then she cooked a special Sunday lunch, even though it wasn't Sunday, with roast chicken and apple crumble. The table was laid with all the best china and her best tablecloth, and she'd done her hair and put on powder and lipstick. Even Uncle George looked less like an old scarecrow than usual. He'd slicked down his hair and put a tie on. Grandfather wasn't there and no one would tell me where he was. Mum just tapped her nose at me and smiled mysteriously. Barry said he knew what it was all about but he wasn't going to tell me. So I pretended I didn't care anyway, which upset him a bit, which I shouldn't have. He was only trying to keep the surprise. And when the surprise came it was supreme, just supreme.

When we heard the dogs barking outside, I knew then it would be Adie. I was sure of it. I ran outside, but it wasn't an American jeep; it was a car, Grandfather's old Ford, still dusty from being kept in the barn. Someone was waving at me. I couldn't see who it was, not at first. Then he opened the door and got out. But he wasn't wearing an American uniform. It was a British uniform, with stripes on the right way up. Dad! Dad in his beret! Dad was home! "Hello Lil," he said. "Remember me?" I ran to him and we hugged there in the farmyard with Uncle George's dog chewing at the tyres of Grandfather's car. Then Mum did her hugging and cried a lot, and even Uncle George looked as if he was crying too as he shook Dad's hand. When I looked round a few minutes later to introduce Barry, he'd gone. He was there sitting beside me at lunch but he wasn't his usual chatty self, and he didn't eat much either, which wasn't at all like him. It was the *best* lunch. Dad ate as if he hadn't eaten at all in the two years he'd been gone.

He said right at the start he wasn't going to say a word about Africa and Italy and the army. He only wanted to know about home, about the farm and the evacuation, and how we'd all managed. We told him everything about the move, about Adie and Harry and about the Slapton Sands Hotel and Tips. He said how sorry he was and kissed me, which was nice because I knew he'd never really liked Tips all that much.

He did try to talk to Barry, but Barry had gone all shy and quiet and wouldn't say a word. After a while Barry asked to be excused and went out. I couldn't understand why he was behaving like he was until Mum said it. "He lost his father," she told Dad quietly. "In the RAF, over Dunkirk, wasn't it, Lil?" I felt so bad, so stupid not to have realised. I had my father back, but Barry could never have his back. I went out and found him sitting looking at the sea. He didn't want to talk. He didn't want to look at me even. He did want me to stay though, I could tell. I sat down beside him, and we said nothing to one another for a long time, which is what only true friends can do.

Barry cheered up that evening, but I wasn't that happy because Mum told me I had to move out of our room so Dad could sleep there. I'm sleeping on the sofa in the sitting room until Dad goes. He says he's got five days' leave. It's not so bad though, because with any luck I'll get to stay up late every night. They can't exactly make me go to bed, can they, if I'm down here? And anyway, it's not so bad, I've got the fire to look at and keep me warm.

I know I shouldn't say this. I shouldn't even have thought it. But I did. When Dad arrived, and I saw it wasn't an American jeep, I remember I felt a little disappointed. When I saw it was Dad I was happy, but I was sad too at the same time because it wasn't Adie. That's wrong, I know it is. But I am pleased my dad's back here and alive and well. I've missed him so much. I know that now he's come home. We're a real family again. He's thinner than he was and he's lost some of his hair, but I won't tell him that. He wouldn't like it.

Monday, March 20th 1944

I had to say goodbye to Dad before I went off to school this morning. He walked Barry and me to the end of the lane to meet the school bus, with Barry wearing his beret. He loves Dad's beret. Dad was in his uniform again, the first time he'd put it back on since the day he'd arrived, and I was very proud of him when the other children saw him. He's got three stripes on his arm, which means he's a sergeant and can tell other soldiers what to do. I think I didn't cry because I was even more proud than I was sad. He told me I had to be good. "I'll be home again soon, Lil," he said. "You look after your mum for me, and be good. The war'll be over before you know it." Barry handed him his beret. Dad ruffled his hair and we got on the bus. We ran to the back seat. Dad was getting smaller and smaller in the distance. Soon, all too soon, he was gone altogether. Then I did cry. But I looked hard out of the window so that no one would know.

It's been so strange having Dad back home. Somehow there didn't seem to be a proper place for him in the house. He spent most of the time with Grandfather and Uncle George on the farm, mending all the machinery, and a whole afternoon tinkering with the tractor engine with Barry, who loves getting his hands oily. Once he went off drinking in the pub with Uncle George and the others in the Home Guard, a sort of welcome home party I think it was, but we couldn't go of course because we're not allowed in pubs. Mum was so happy when he first came home, but then I'd see her gazing at him out of the kitchen window, and I knew what she was thinking. As the days passed and Dad's leave got shorter and shorter, we were all thinking the same thing. We didn't laugh like we had before. We were just waiting for the moment he had to leave, so we couldn't enjoy him being there as much as we should have done. It hung like a shadow over us. Now he's gone, and it's as if he's never been home at all. I'm going to pray for him every night he's away, starting right now, I won't miss once. Cross my heart and hope to die.

Wednesday, March 29th 1944

When we go to school now, we see more and more soldiers. Mostly they're Yanks, but some of them are ours too. We see them in lorries and in tanks, we see them marching along. They're putting up whole villages of tents all over the place. Every time I see a black soldier I look to see if it's Adie or Harry. I haven't seen Adie for ages now. I expect they've been doing lots more of their landing exercises. I know he's all right because Uncle George said he saw him only yesterday on patrol with Harry along the perimeter wire. Uncle George said he'd asked them to come and visit us again sometime. I hope they do. I really hope they do.

Thursday, April 20th 1944

The day of the Great Hot-dog Feast. That's what I'm calling today.

Barry and I were running up the lane, coming back from school. We were racing one another and I was winning, as usual, when we heard a car coming up behind us. It was Adie and Harry in their jeep. They said they were just coming to visit. Harry was carrying a bunch of daffodils. They gave us a lift home, which was good fun, but what happened next was SUPREME.

They were sausages really, but they called them hot dogs and they brought dozens of them. I've never seen so many sausages in my life. They said you just stick them between slices of bread and pour on tomato ketchup, and they brought that along too. So we had a great hot-dog feast, all of us together in the kitchen, and in the middle of the table were the daffodils Adie and Harry had given Mum. Barry said it was the best meal of his life.

He ate six! And got ketchup all over his face. I could only manage three. But they were supreme!

We only mentioned Tips once, when Uncle George's cat came in rubbing up against my leg and looking for a sausage himself. I told Adie what had happened, how Tips had gone off and about the hotel being blown up. He knew about the hotel, but he told me I wasn't to worry. "She'll come home," Adie said. "That cat's a real survivor, sure as my name is Adolphus T. Madison." And I said I wasn't so sad any more because I hadn't really thought about her since Dad came home, which was true.

Everyone talked about Dad a lot, and Mum told them she didn't know where he was exactly, but maybe he'd be part of the invasion too when it happened, and how maybe they'd meet up in France one day. And we all did a cheers to victory,

Barry and me in soda pop, which they'd brought along, and which is like a sort of American lemonade. It's nice, but not as nice as our lemonade. And the grown-ups did their cheers in beer, which Adie and Harry brought along too. They'd brought along the whole hot-dog feast – everything.

Adie's so tall he can't stand up straight in the sitting room without hitting his head. He keeps knocking his head and laughing at himself. And when Adie laughs, everyone laughs, the whole house seems to laugh. They didn't just bring us sausages, they brought us real happiness. Then they drove away into the darkness. Now they're gone the house seems empty and quiet. Barry's been sick, but he says it was worth it.

Friday, April 28th 1944

There was a thunderstorm out at sea last night. It woke me up. I knelt up on my bed and watched the lightening from my window. Mum slept through it, so did everyone else, but I heard it. I didn't imagine it. Tips used to hate thunderstorms. She'd burrow down my bed and hide. But they never frightened me, until this one. Or maybe it was the sudden blackness and silence which followed it that frightened me. I don't know. I hoped Adie and Harry weren't out in it doing one of their practice landings.

In school today Mrs Blumfeld read us a story. It was all about America. It's called *Little House in the Big Woods*. I like it a lot, but the people in it don't talk at all like Adie and Harry, not the way Mrs Blumfeld reads it anyway.

Uncle George's radio has gone wrong again. All you can hear is whistles and crackling. He's really cross but he still sits there all evening trying to listen to it, banging it from time to time, but all he gets is more whistling, more crackling. Barry and I got the giggles when Barry imitated Uncle George's grumpy face, and Mum told us off.

Monday, May 1st 1944

I wish today had never happened, that I'd never woken up this morning. It was all perfectly normal to start with: breakfast with Barry and Mum, off to school, lessons, playtime, lunch, more lessons, then the bus home. We walked into the kitchen and there was Adie sitting at the table with Mum. I knew there was something wrong at once. He was looking up at me as if he didn't want me to be there. Then he looked away.

It was Mum who told us. "It's Harry," she said quietly. "Adie came to tell us: he's been killed."

When Adie spoke, his voice was filled with tears. "We was told we gotta keep it quiet," he said. "But I ain't gonna keep it quiet, not for nobody. There's hundreds of us dead out there. What they gonna tell their folks back home? I tell you what they gonna say. Training accident or some such thing. But I was there and I knows. I knows what happened. I seen it with my own eyes. We had no way of fighting back, no way of defending ourselves. There were no one out there watching our backs, and that ain't right. That just ain't right." He cried then and couldn't go on. So Mum went on for him. She told us that three nights ago, the soldiers had been a few miles off shore in their ships, waiting to come in and do another practice landing on Slapton Sands, when suddenly out of nowhere came these German E-boats. The ships were like sitting ducks. They were torpedoed. They didn't stand a chance. They were all sunk. Hundreds of men were lost. Some of the soldiers, like Adie, did get picked up – but Harry wasn't one of them.

Mum gave him a cup of tea after that, and afterwards Barry and I walked him to the end of the lane.

"There's something I wanna tell you," he said. "Harry and me, we talked plenty. We was talking one day about what we was doing over here fighting in this white man's war. You know what he said? He said, 'I know why I'm doing it, because we ain't going to be no one's slaves never again, that's why. We got our freedom and we're not gonna let no one take it away. We gonna keep it.' That's what he said. But when I go over there to France, I ain't gonna be fighting for no one's freedom. I'm gonna be fighting for Harry, and they'd better watch out, because now I'm mad, I'm fighting mad." And as he put on his helmet he managed a smile. "Harry got no family back home. He told me after we was here last time that he reckoned you were about the only white folks that ever treated him like family. Right now that's just about how I feel too." Adie walked away from us and never looked back.

As we watched I wanted to run after him and hug him to me and never let him go. I wanted to tell him I loved him and that I'll love him to the day I die. Because I do. I love him more than lemon sherberts, more than mint humbugs, more than I love Tips or Mum or Dad, more than all of those put together. And that's the truth.

On the way home I picked a daffodil. I've put it in my diary on this page. So it'll always be here marking the day Harry died, and the day when I first knew I loved Adie.

Wednesday, May 10th 1944

Adie still hasn't come back to see us again. I've been hoping and hoping every day. I wonder if he ever will. I can't stop thinking of him walking away down the lane, and that maybe it's the last time I'll ever see him. Mrs Blumfeld keeps saying the invasion must happen soon, any day now, she says – when the weather's right. They've got to wait till the weather's right. It's rough out at sea today. I hope it stays rough for ever, and then Adie won't have to go on the invasion, and he'll be safe.

I helped Barry and Mum pull off a calf this afternoon. The calf was walking inside ten minutes. I've seen lots of lambs born, lots of calves, and each time it surprises me how quickly they can get up and walk on their wobbly legs. What takes us a year or more, they can do inside an hour.

Mum's a bit down. It's because she hasn't had a letter from Dad since he left. We don't even know where he is. We think he's in England still, but we don't really know. We were kneeling there in the field, watching the calf trying out his first skip and falling over himself, and Barry was laughing. But Mum and me weren't laughing because our minds were elsewhere. If Barry hadn't been there I think I'd have told her there and then: "I know what it feels like, Mum, to miss someone you really really love."

I can't tell Barry that I love Adie, that's for sure, because he's too young and he wouldn't understand, and even if he did understand he'd be upset. He's never said it, but I know he wants me to be his girlfriend. I never will be, not now. Barry's more like a brother to me, more like a friend, a really good friend. With Adie, it's different, so completely different.

Saturday, May 20th 1944

Mrs Turner has come to stay, Barry's mum (she likes us to call her Ivy). Last Tuesday she just turned up out of the blue, to give Barry a nice birthday surprise, she said – that's in two days time. She gave him a surprise all right. She gave us all a surprise. We got back from school and there she was sitting with Mum at the kitchen table, her suitcase beside her. She hugged Barry so tight and for so long that I thought his eyes might pop out, and she pinched his cheek, which I could see he didn't like at all. She's got lots of powder on her face and bright scarlet lipstick, which Barry's always wiping off his face after she kisses him, and that's very often. And her eyebrows are pencilled on, not real, just like Marlene Dietrich in the films, Mum says.

Barry hasn't said much since she's been here, nor has anyone else. No one can get a word in edgeways. His mum never stops talking. She could

"talk the hind legs off a ruddy donkey" – that's
what Grandfather says. And she smokes all the
time too, "like a ruddy chimbley" – Grandfather
says that too. Ivy's nice though. I like her. She came
with presents for everyone, and told us again and

again how kind we'd been to look after Barry for her. All through supper tonight she told us story after story about the Blitz in London, about the air-raid sirens, running to shelters and sleeping at nights down in the underground stations. She talks in a "townie" accent just like Barry does, only a lot louder and for a lot longer. She's very proud of her big red London bus. "I'm tellin' you. Ain't nothin' goin' to stop my number seventy-four from gettin' where she's goin'," she said this evening. "'Oles in the road, busted bridges, tumbled-down houses. They can send over all the hexplodin' doodahs they like. Will they stop my bus from gettin' where it's goin'? Not bloomin' likely, that's what I say."

Barry tries to stop her talking from time to time, but it's no use. In the end he just goes out and lets her get on with it. He spends even more time now out on the farm with Grandfather and Uncle George. Barry's mum makes no bones about it: she doesn't like the country one little bit, and farms in particular. "Smelly places. All that mud. All them cows. And the bloomin' birds wakin' you up in the mornin'." Yesterday she was washing up at the sink with Mum after supper when all at once she burst into tears. "What is it?" Mum asked, putting an arm around her.

"It's all that green," she said, pointing out of the window. "It's just green everywhere. And there's no buildin's. And it's so empty. I 'ate green. I don't know why, I just 'ate it."

She hardly ever goes out, just stays in the kitchen, smoking and drinking tea. Mum likes her a lot because she's good company for her and because Barry's mum loves to help out. She likes to be busy, fetching and carrying, scrubbing floors, ironing and polishing. She's black-leaded Uncle George's stove for him so he's happy too. Barry never actually says he wants her to go home, but I can feel he does. I don't think he's ashamed of her exactly, but you can tell he's uncomfortable with her around. He either wants to be at home with her in London, or down here with us, but not both. That's what I think anyway.

One good thing is that she's always teasing Uncle George, and no one else dares do that, about the holes in the elbows of his jacket, about how scruffy he looks. She sat him down a couple of days ago and cut his hair for him. She mended his jacket for him. And when Uncle George grumbles on as he does, about how he can never find anything these days with all of us living on top of him, how he used to have a bit of peace and quiet before we came, she just laughs at him.

"Go on," Ivy said (it sounded more like "garn"). "You'll miss 'em when they've gone back 'ome again, you know you will, you grumpy old codger you."

Surprisingly Uncle George didn't argue with her. He thought for a while and then he said, "Maybe I will, maybe I will." I think he really meant it.

Monday, May 22nd 1944

Barry's eleventh birthday. Barry's mum had brought down his birthday cake. She'd saved up her ration coupons for weeks and weeks. "I made it special," she said. And it was very special: fruit cake, with marzipan and royal icing with his name written on it in blue piping. Barry blew out the candles and closed his eyes to make his wish. Ivy had tears in her eyes and was trying not to cry. I think they were both wishing for the same thing, for the impossible: for Barry's father to be coming home.

I'll miss Ivy when she goes tomorrow. I think we all will. She makes us smile. She turns off Uncle George's crackling radio and we talk. She laughs a lot and never pretends. I like that. She means everything she says. I like people who mean what they say – a bit like Barry really. But I wish she wouldn't call me "ducky".

Friday, May 26th 1944

Mum's not been at all well. She's been coughing a lot for days now. She's very pale. The doctor came yesterday and said she had to have bed rest until she stops her coughing. Grandfather said that I could stay off school and look after her for a day or two, and help around the house with the cooking and cleaning. Barry said he'd stay home to help too, but Grandfather wouldn't hear of it and sent him off to school. Barry's not very pleased. He shouldn't grumble though. He's had lots of days off school to help out on the farm, specially at lambing time.

Mum had a letter from Dad today, so that cheered her up. He says he's somewhere in the south of England. He can't say where. Mum thinks he'll be going on the invasion when it happens. Maybe he'll meet up with Adie like we hoped he would. She keeps all his letters by her bed all the time, beside his photo.

This afternoon I went for a walk on my own up to the top of the hill. The larks were flying so high I could only hear them, but I couldn't see them. I did see the buzzards, two of them, floating on the air over the trees, mewing. For a moment they sounded just like Tips. Then I looked out to sea and saw the ships in the bay, dozens and dozens of them. I've never seen so many. It's the invasion. It must be. They're not gathered there for nothing, are they? There's one other thing I noticed today

while I was up there. It wasn't only the sounds of the countryside I could hear about me. There was always a dull droning. I couldn't think what it was at first. Then I knew. It was the rumble of engines, jeeps, lorries, tanks. It was the rumble of war. I stood on the top of the hill with the wind blowing in my face, smelling the sea and all I could think of was Adie. I said a prayer out loud, then I shouted it into the wind. "Please, God, let him come and see me before he goes to the war. Please, God. Please."

Tuesday, June 6th 1944

We heard it on the radio. They've gone. The invasion began this morning. Adie's gone. Dad too probably. D-day they're calling it. I don't know why. We all knew something was going on before we heard it on the radio. Before dawn there was a distant thundering and roaring out at sea. Out of my window I could see flashes all along the horizon, and I knew then it wasn't just another thunderstorm. There must have been thousands of

guns firing at the same time. And when Barry and me ran up over the fields after breakfast and looked out to sea, we saw all the ships had gone. So it was no surprise when on the radio this evening it said that we had landed all along the French coast: Americans, British, Canadians, French, all sorts. Uncle George said we'd show the Germans now. He and Mum drank too much cider together and danced a jig around the kitchen to celebrate and Uncle George's mad dog danced too, barking his silly head off. To start with, Barry and me sat and watched them. Everyone was laughing.

Mum still coughs when she laughs, but she's much better. But in the end we got up and danced with them. We did a conga round and round the table, till we all got puffed out. Then Mum gave Barry and me two mint humbugs each and some lemonade, to celebrate. Uncle George and Mum had a whisky each and we all clinked our glasses. "To victory," Uncle George said.

Grandfather came in from milking later and Mum told him what we'd heard on the radio. He said nothing, but went to wash his hands in the sink. Then all he said was, "Poor beggars. Poor beggars."

Mum said when she came up to bed a few minutes ago that today was the beginning of the end of the war, that Dad would be back soon, and then we could go back home to the farm and everything would be as it was before. But I don't think anything will ever be like it was again. Nothing stays the same, does it? Nothing is ever like it was, is it?

All I can think about as I write this is that Adie

might be lying out there tonight on some French beach, dead or wounded, and I'll never know, because no one will ever tell me because no one will ever know that we knew each other. I try closing my eyes and picturing him in my head. I try so hard to see him not dead and not wounded either. I try to see him alive and smiling at me. Whatever happens to him, wherever he is, that's how I'm going to remember him, for ever.

I know I should be thinking of Dad too, and I am. I'm trying. I'm thinking of them both now. I'm praying for them too.

This is me writing now, Boowie. This is your grandma. I wrote lots more in my diary after this but none of it is very interesting, and anyway the mice got some of it years later when my diary books were stored in a box up in the attic — mice or squirrels, I can't be sure. There are only two more entries I wanted to show you because they finish the whole supremely amazing story, in so far as my story finishes at all. And if you don't understand quite what I mean by that then you'll find out soon enough, but not until after the whole of the story has unfolded. Curiouser and curiouser…!

Thursday, October 5th 1944

My birthday and we've moved back home. It should have been the best birthday present I ever had. I was longing for today. And now it's come and I should be happy, but I'm not. This house isn't my home. It's an empty shell stacked with furniture, tea chests everywhere, and it's damp. When we arrived the front door was hanging off its hinges, so anyone could have been in and out, and by the look of it they have been too. It's a real mess. There's black mould on the ceiling, green in some places, and there are dead birds and leaves everywhere. The wallpaper's falling off above the chimney in the sitting room, and half a dozen of the windows are broken. The rain's come in and rotted the windowsill in my bedroom. The ceiling in Grandfather's room has come down in one corner: there's a hole in the roof where the slates have been blasted away by some shell.

The gutters are full of grass and one drainpipe

has fallen down into the garden and smashed the greenhouse. Not that you can call it a garden, not any more. You can hardly see a flower. Grass has grown up everywhere. You can't even see where the flowerbeds and the vegetable garden were. The granary must have taken a direct hit from a shell because there's nothing left of it but rubble.

Barry and me went off on a walk around the farm. There's nettles and docks head-high wherever you look. But the worst of it is that it's all so quiet. Only Grandfather seems truly happy to be home. "Never you mind," Grandfather said this evening, as we sat around the table in the kitchen in gloomy silence, "once we bring the animals back tomorrow, the place'll come alive, you'll see. We'll soon put it all right. Spick-and-span in no time. Few hens about the place and they'll cackle loud enough to drive out any quiet." I hope he's right. At least I'm back in my own room, even if it doesn't feel like it yet. All I've got so far is my bed, my chair and my lamp. My room smells. The whole house smells.

PS I can't believe this! I just finished writing my diary, and was reaching out to blow out the lamp, when I noticed some writing on the wall by the window, in pencil. This is what it says:

January 10th 1944. Harry and Adie were here looking for Tips. Welcome home Lily!

I just keep reading it over and over again. I can't stop crying and I don't know whether it's because I'm happy or I'm sad. I'm both. I'm not going to tell anyone about this, not tonight. It was written to me, so tonight I'm going to keep it to myself. I'll tell the others in the morning. I have to look at it again and again to believe it is real.

Friday, October 6th 1944

Supreme! Supreme! I feel supreme all over, because just about the best thing that could happen, has happened, and it happened at breakfast time.

I wondered where I was when I first woke up this morning. The window was in the wrong place. I was lying in bed, trying to work it all out, when I saw the writing on the wall. Then I remembered everything. I was home! I jumped out of bed and called everyone in to my room to show them the message Adie and Harry had left. Of course I told them as if I'd only just discovered it. Grandfather wasn't there. He'd already gone up to Uncle George's to milk the cows. All we talked about at breakfast was the writing on the wall, but we were in a hurry because Mum said we had to be up at Uncle George's as quick as we could, "lickety-split" she said, to help fetch home the cows after milking.

Anyway, we were washing the dishes when the

back door opened, all by itself it seemed, and in she came, meowing and purring all at the same time, wandering under the table, in amongst the chair legs, tail quivering with pleasure. Tips! Tips alive! Tips back from the dead! We were all crying, Barry too, and he doesn't even like cats. I put down some milk for her and she lapped till she'd licked the bowl clean. She's a lot thinner than she was, and there's a scratch on her face which wasn't there before. But she's definitely Tips, my Tips, green eyes, white paws and all her black patches in the right place. And she purrs the same too.

Mum said I didn't have to go with them to fetch the animals home, that she and Grandfather and Barry could manage without me. So all I've done today is cuddle Tips. I've played with her, fed her and cuddled her again. I think I gave her ten months' worth of cuddles in one day. She's come home, just like Adie said she would. I've looked back in my diary to be sure. These are exactly his words: "She'll come home. That cat's a real survivor, sure as my name is Adolphus T. Madison." So I've decided that from now on she's always going to be called Adolphus Tips. I asked her first of course, and she purred. So I know she's happy about it. Mind you, she's been purring nonstop ever since she came home! I think she's happy because she's got an important-sounding name, and she likes to feel important. I keep saying it, to get myself used to it, getting her used to it. Adolphus Tips. Adolphus Tips. It makes me smile every time I say it out loud, because it sounds so funny, and because every time I say it I think of Adie.

Just now I touched the writing on the wall before I turned down the lamp. I'm going to do that every night to bring him luck over in France. And I'm going to pray for him too, then maybe he'll come back like Tips has, like Adolphus Tips has.

And now, Boowie, over sixty years later, here's the beginning of the end of the story.

Adie didn't come back. But there has hardly been a day since I haven't thought about him, and about Adolphus Tips too. She was already quite an old cat by the time we found one another again, and she aged quickly after her miraculous return. I think that her struggle for survival on her own must have taken a lot out of her, and giving birth to all those kittens too. She died peacefully three years later and I buried her in the garden.

Gradually the people moved back into the cottages and farms all around us. As you can imagine, there had been a lot of destruction. Hardly a single building had survived unscathed and many were in ruins. The farms and farmyards were infested with weeds and rats, and there were rabbits everywhere, thousands of them. We ate a lot of rabbit stew! For a while it was a sad place to be, but bit by bit things improved. The houses were repaired, the farms tidied up. The church had been hit too, one of the walls blown out, so we couldn't use it for a while. I remember the first time the bells rang again. It was to celebrate the end of the war in 1945.

That was the year Dad came home, and the year the village school opened again. And it was the year we got our generator too. Dad had worked a lot on generators in the army, so he installed it himself. We were one of the first houses in the village to have our own electricity. Dad was always very proud of that. Later on, generators became his business. He took over one of the barns as his workshop and he supplied generators all over the country, all over the world. Mum and Grandfather and I went on running the farm together and we were quite happy to be doing it.

After the war was over Barry went back home to London, back to his mother. He wrote to me for a while, but then we lost touch. One of us didn't reply, I don't remember which. He came back to see us though several years afterwards. He had his new wife with him and wanted her to meet us, and to show her the farm I suppose. I remember I was even a little jealous. He still smiled the same, was still very sweet and kind. He told us over tea that his stay with us during the war had been the happiest time of his childhood. He's living out in Australia now near a place called Armidale in New South Wales. He became a sheep farmer. After his time with us down on the farm, he never wanted to be anything other than a farmer. We exchange photos of our grandchildren at Christmas. I hope to go and visit him one day. We'll see.

As you know, Boowie, Mrs Blumfeld never went back to Holland after the war, but stayed on in our village as the school teacher. You came with me to see her once or twice, do you remember? She's in the graveyard now, not far from Grandfather and Uncle George, and Mum and Dad too, and now your Grandpa as well. I keep all their graves as tidy as I can, and I often put flowers there too, snowdrops, primroses, bluebells, daffodils, fuchsia, whatever is in season, whatever I can find in the garden. Sometimes we've done it together, Boowie, haven't we?

Now to the end of my story. It was about three years ago. You had just gone back home, I remember, after spending your holidays with your grandpa and me. I was going for my usual walk along the beach, past the place where the old hotel had once been, when I saw a couple of men standing at the water's edge looking out to sea. I remember thinking it was strange because they looked a little out of place, not dressed for the beach at all. As you know, you can hear someone coming on those pebbles from a long way away. They must have heard me because they turned round to look at me at the same time. Both of them were very tall, and both were black. One looked much older than the other. He had white hair and was carrying a bunch of flowers. Maybe this was something I'd always believed would happen, because I knew who it was the moment I set eyes on him. It wasn't only my eyes that told me. It was my heart too. But he didn't recognise me. They turned away again, and as I watched, both of them began scattering the flowers into the sea, throwing them as far out as they could, which wasn't very far, so they soon floated in again on the waves and washed up on the beach. I knew the flowers were for Harry.

I waited a while before I approached them, not

wishing to disturb the moment.

"Adie?" I said. He turned and looked at me. It was him! It really was him. "Adolphus T. Madison," I went on. "That's T for Thomas, Private First Class, US Army?"

Then he smiled the smile I remembered. "Lily?" he said. And we each took each other's hands, unable to say another word.

So Adie and his son — he's called him Harry — came back to the bungalow and had tea with your grandpa and me. In between the scones and the macaroons Adie and I told one another the stories of our lives — there was a fair bit to catch up on, as you can imagine. We had a wonderful time together that day. Your grandpa took to Adie at once because Adie talked to him as if he wasn't in a wheelchair, as if he wasn't ill, and he always liked that, as you know. It was whilst we were talking that Harry told me that Adie had been wanting to make this trip all his life, to remember his old friend Harry and to visit the farm again where Lily, the little girl with the cat lived, and where they'd been made to feel so welcome.

Harry had grown up with the story all his life. Adie's wife had died a year or so before, and he didn't want to leave it any longer. "So we decided we'd just pack our bags and come right over," Adie said. "Say, d'you remember that day we came visiting with the hot dogs?" We laughed out loud then as we recalled the Great Hot-dog Feast and Barry's face covered in ketchup from ear to ear. I told him that Tips had come back home in the end just like he said she would, and that I'd renamed her Adolphus Tips. He said that it made him feel "real proud" to hear that.

They drove away after tea was over and went to see the farm on their way back to London. I should have liked to have gone with them of course, but your grandpa would have been upset if I'd left him alone again so soon after my daily walk. But Adie and I wrote to one another after that, often. He sent flowers for your grandpa's funeral and then wrote to me afterwards saying that if ever I'd like to visit them in Atlanta I'd be more than welcome.

So I went, Boowie, and that's where I am now, in Atlanta, in America. I don't think the two of us have stopped talking since the day I arrived — we have a lot of time to make up. And so when Adie asked me a week ago now, it seemed the most natural thing in the world to say yes. We got married last Tuesday. Second time around and I've married my childhood sweetheart. The church was full to bursting, and you never heard such wonderful singing in all your life. They sing with such joy over here, as if they really mean every word, every note. So I'm now Mrs Madison, and as soon as the honeymoon's over I'm bringing him home with me to live in Slapton. We'll be having our honeymoon in New York — neither of us have ever been there — and then we'll be flying back to London next Saturday evening. We arrive at Heathrow, Terminal Four at half past seven. I'm longing for you to meet him, Boowie. You'll like him, I know you will. I hope everyone else does too. Be there if you can.

I was there of course. We all were: uncles and aunties, the whole family. Some of them were still upset by the surprise of it all, but everyone was curious, me most of all. So we were all waiting for them at Heathrow, ready with confetti – that was my idea – as they came out of customs.

She looked so small beside him. They were holding hands and smiling like two cats that had got the cream and were blissfully happy to be sharing it. And then I was shaking Adie's hand. "Hi, there," he said, beaming down at me from a great height. "I reckon you've got to be Boowie. Yep. You're just like someone I used to know a long, long time ago, except you're a boy, of course, and you ain't got no pigtails."

After a while Grandma led me away, her arm around my shoulder.

"What do you think, Boowie?" she whispered.

"Supreme," I said. "Just supreme."

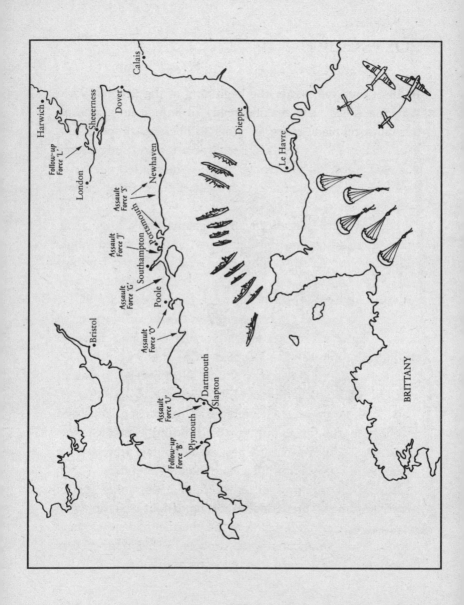

Harwich

Calais

Dover

Sheeerness

Follow-up
Force 'L'

London

Dieppe

Newhaven

Le Havre

Assault
Force 'S'

Portsmouth

Assault
Force 'J'

Southampton

Assault
Force 'G'

Poole

Bristol

Assault
Force 'O'

Dartmouth

Slapton

Assault
Force 'U'

Plymouth

Follow-up
Force 'B'

BRITTANY

POSTSCRIPT

In 1943, four years after the beginning of the Second World War, the Allies were making ready to launch an attack on German occupied France, in order to liberate Europe at last from Hitler and the Nazis. A seaborne attack on such a large scale had never been attempted before. The soldiers needed to practise, to exercise, and so they needed the training ground to do it.

The southern part of England became like a huge army camp, as the invasion force gathered and rehearsed. Many coastal areas had to be cleared so that simulated landings from the sea could take place, so that the soldiers were prepared when the time for the real invasion came.

The area around Slapton Sands in Devon was evacuated because the beach there was similar to the landing beaches in Normandy, across the English Channel. About 3000 inhabitants were given just a few short weeks to gather everything they had and move out.

Of course the disruption caused great hardship, and damage to the area during the landing exercises was extensive. There were casualties too of course, amongst the soldiers – and in Slapton they were mostly Americans.

During Operation Tiger in April of 1944, ships full of American troops preparing to be landed at Slapton were surprised by German E-boats in the channel and sunk. Many hundreds of Americans were drowned. This tragedy was deliberately kept secret for many years afterwards.

Then, on the morning of June 6th 1944, came D-day, as it was called, when the Allies landed on the French coast and fought their way off the beaches and inland, liberating French villages and towns as they went. Eleven months of hard fighting later, Germany surrendered and the Second World War came to an end.